Hashim Ali Y5.

Dear Hashim,

THE
Lizzie AND Belle
MYSTERIES

PORTRAITS AND POISON

All the best,

J.T. Williams.

First published in Great Britain in 2023 by Farshore

An imprint of HarperCollins*Publishers*
1 London Bridge Street, London SE1 9GF

farshore.co.uk

HarperCollins*Publishers*
Macken House, 39/40 Mayor Street Upper,
Dublin 1, D01 C9W8

Text copyright © 2023 Joanna Brown and Storymix Limited
Illustrations © 2023 Simone Douglas
Illustrations pages 64, 138, 240, 241 © Shutterstock

ISBN 978 0 0084 8528 3
Printed and bound in the UK using 100% renewable electricity
at CPI Group (UK) Ltd
1

Stay safe online. Any website addresses listed in this book are
correct at the time of going to print. However, Farshore is not
responsible for content hosted by third parties. Please be aware
that online content can be subject to change and websites can
contain content that is unsuitable for children. We advise that
all children are supervised when using the internet.

MIX
Paper | Supporting
responsible forestry
FSC™ C007454

This book is produced from independently certified FSC™ paper
to ensure responsible forest management.

For more information visit: www.harpercollins.co.uk/green

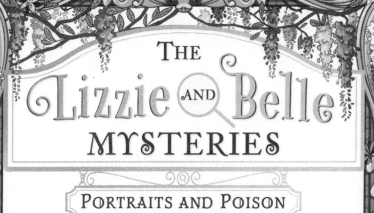

THE
Lizzie AND Belle
MYSTERIES

PORTRAITS AND POISON

J.T. WILLIAMS

ILLUSTRATED BY SIMONE DOUGLAS

KENWOOD
HOUSE

HAMPSTEAD HEATH

ST GILES

THEATRE
ROYAL

ROYAL
ACADEMY

COVENT
GARDEN
MARKET

LEICESTER
FIELDS

ST JAMES'S PARK

ST MARGARET'S
CHURCH

WESTMINSTER
ABBEY

SANCHO'S
TEA SHOP

THE DOG
AND DUCK PUB

TOWER
OF LONDON

ST PAUL'S
CATHEDRAL

RIVERSIDE
SOUTH

LONDON

Prologue

What does it mean to be part of a family?

How does it feel to truly belong to someone?

The words 'mother', 'father', 'sister', 'brother', 'daughter' and 'son' conjure different feelings for each of us, depending on our own experience.

Not everyone even has such people in their life.

I should know, for such is my case.

For those of you that have not met me before, I'm Belle. Dido Elizabeth Belle, great-niece of the Mansfield family.

I have not seen my parents for several years now.

For reasons unknown to me, when I was just an infant, my mother and father handed me over to the care of my great-uncle and aunt: Lord and Lady Mansfield. I live with them here at Kenwood House, a magnificent mansion on Hampstead Heath, an oasis of glorious greenery on the northernmost edge of London.

The newspapers don't quite know what to make of me. To them, I'm a puzzle. A member of a British aristocratic family with African heritage, born out of wedlock. In their columns they call me 'mysterious heiress', 'illegitimate niece' and 'adopted relative'.

But I have learned that it is best not to let others define you. I prefer to describe myself as a bookworm, would-be writer and, more recently, detective.

There I am, at the centre of a painting. The Mansfield-Sancho Portrait. Two families captured together on canvas.

I'm the one in the cream satin dress.

That's Aunt Betty standing behind me. Lady Elizabeth Murray, Countess of Mansfield. The great organiser of the household, she commands an army of staff in a house of more than fifty rooms, if you count the servants' quarters. Don't be fooled by her stern expression: though strict in character and obsessed with social etiquette, at heart she is a kind, soft soul. Some say the secret to her contentment is her lifelong love for her husband.

May I present the Earl of Mansfield, Lord Chief Justice, the most powerful judge and lawmaker in England? Hence the scarlet robes of court and the flowing wig. Lord Mansfield is most famous for his rulings on slavery cases – some say his decisions are moving us towards the abolition of slavery once and for all.

To me, he is simply dear Uncle William.

My father is their nephew, Sir John Lindsay, a captain of the Royal Navy. He's not in this family portrait because he doesn't live with us. I can see him clear as day in his coat with the gold edges, his brown hair swept back from his forehead, his serious dark eyes staring back at me. But most of his life is spent at sea; if it were not for the picture of him that hangs in the Great Library of our house, I would not know his face at all.

No one talks to me about my mother, but I think of her every day.

Maria Bell, a young African woman whom my father met on a slaving ship in the Atlantic Ocean near Hispaniola. It has been years since I have seen her. And the only picture I have is the one stamped in my memory, but fading fast. A small, slender, graceful woman with an enchanting smile, her hair cascading down her back in long braids tipped with cowrie shells. It is almost a decade since I watched laughter spark lights in her round brown eyes as she lifted me into the sky above her head, then planted me on her hip, where I sat, a constant companion, breathing in the warm sweet perfume of her neck, my thumb in my mouth.

According to Uncle William's account, I was born in London and lived with my mother for a time in a small room by the docks before she brought me to Kenwood.

Kenwood.

More of a palace than a home, it was a house to get lost in. I felt like a mouse in a maze.

You see, I was a tender child.

Timid, meek, unsure of what life held for me.

Over time, in Aunt Betty and Uncle William's care, and with the guidance of governesses, I learned to read and write, to sing, to dance, to recite poetry, to play the piano, to speak French, and to ride horses. Such is the life of an eighteenth-century gentlewoman. But it was a sheltered existence. For many years I knew little of the world beyond Kenwood.

Now, however, a new fire burns in my belly and emboldens my blood.

I feel as though I could take on the world!

What made the difference? I hear you ask. How did you come by this new-found courage? The answer fills me with joy. I lived so long without it, I thought it would never come. The greatest gift a girl could ask for.

True friendship.

Readers, may I introduce – Lizzie Sancho!

The girl standing next to me: the one in the breeches, surrounded by her extraordinary family. My bright and brilliant friend. She is an inspiration to me! Curious and courageous, determined and daring. Her parents, Ann and Ignatius, run Sancho's Tea Shop in Westminster. You may know it: it's a café come literary salon where people gather to catch up with the latest news over a cup of tea or hot chocolate. Sancho's is also one of the key meeting places for the Sons and Daughters of Africa – an organisation of radical rebels committed to the total emancipation of African people. Freedom fighters extraordinaire.

Lizzie lives at the shop with her mother and father, baby brother Billy and three sisters: Kitty, Mary and Frances.

The Sanchos are the kind of family that would gladly share their last loaf of bread with you.

Frances, the eldest of the 'Sanchonettas', is now officially stepping out with Joshua, our family coachman. Joshua, with Uncle's help, is now learning the law to support the fight for freedom. Lizzie and I are secretly banking on Frances and Joshua being married before the year is out.

Meeting Lizzie has transformed my life. She and I are officially committed to the work of detection. Joined by a sense of justice.

According to Dr Johnson's dictionary, the definition of the word 'detect' is 'to discover', or 'to find out any crime or artifice'.

This is the story of our next case.

Here I have set down the events as I remember them.

Read closely.

Observe objectively.

Leave no detail unexamined.

Perhaps, as my story unfolds, you will resolve for yourselves the who, the how and the why of The Case of the Purloined Portrait.

Chapter One

According to *Portraits and People* magazine, the artist Miss Jane Harry had travelled to England from Kingston, Jamaica, and was studying portraiture under the guidance of Sir Joshua Reynolds, President of the Royal Academy of Artists.

Lizzie and I were sitting cross-legged opposite one another in a window-seat in my bedroom, devouring the latest news on Miss Harry while waiting for her to arrive for the first sitting of our joint family portrait. The rest of Lizzie's family had been shown to guest rooms on the upper floors to ready themselves. Aunt Betty and Uncle William were each in their respective dressing rooms on the ground floor.

It was a buoyant blue midsummer morning, and swathes of pale golden sun beamed in through the high windows, dappling the polished wooden floor in petals of light. I had thrown up the sash of the window we sat in: the violet damask curtains swung dreamily in the morning breeze.

'It says here,' announced Lizzie, poring over a page of *Abolitionist News*, 'that Miss Harry takes her surname from her African mother – Charity Harry – rather than from her English father.'

Lizzie laid down the pamphlet in her lap and eyed me earnestly. I found her features endearingly round: her nose, a soft upturned curve; her cheeks, shiny as apples; her dark brown lips full and expressive. Today, her hair was plaited to her head in an intricate pattern of elaborate zigzags and diamonds: traces of her mother's love in their delicate arrangement.

'Like you, Belle!' she said, passing me the paper.

This common thread between Jane Harry's family story and my own intrigued me. My father's surname, Lindsay, had been denied me; neither had the surname that Aunt and Uncle went by, Murray, ever been considered mine to claim. Being born of unmarried parents in our time was challenge enough. But that my mother and father held such contrasting positions in society . . .

Sadly I knew only too well what wicked whispers and spiteful speculations such family stories encouraged in certain circles. Was this why Miss Harry had sailed halfway around the world from her family and was now striking out on her own, painting portraits professionally? Would I have had the courage to make such a move, I wondered.

'Apparently, she's an heiress,' I said, scanning the page, 'but it doesn't say what she is due to inherit.'

'Here she is!' exclaimed Lizzie, suddenly up on her knees and waving exuberantly out of the window.

Lizzie cut an impressive figure today in her crisp white shirt and royal-blue breeches. She refused what she called the 'fussiness' of women's fashion. 'How am I supposed to run with all that satin bunching up around my legs?' she had once said to me in exasperation. I thought of the row upon row of silk and satin gowns hanging in my own wardrobe and tried to imagine myself asking Aunt Betty the same question. It would not have gone down well.

Outside, a tall elegant young woman was striding up the rain-fresh emerald slope towards Kenwood House, her rich magenta cloak rippling in the breeze. Behind her, beyond the dew-dazzled grass, the wood pond shimmered sweetly in the sunshine. At the top of the hill, the artist stopped and gazed upwards, shielding her eyes from the glare with her hand. Under her right arm, she carried a large black sketchbook. Slung over her shoulder, a bag crammed full of paints, brushes and pencils, like a quiver full of arrows, ready for action!

Lizzie and I raced down the staircase and across the Great Hall, skidding on the newly varnished floor as we rushed to greet our guest. I stopped to compose myself, smoothed down the front of my cream satin dress, patted my chignon and flung open the door just as Miss Harry was lifting her hand to knock.

Caught off guard, the young artist laughed: a charmingly musical ripple of surprise. Her creamy gold skin radiated health; her green eyes sparkled like a cat's on a night walk.

'Thank you, girls! What an astonishingly beautiful house you have here, Belle!' enthused Miss Harry, stepping into the hall and gazing around at the harmonious blue walls, the smooth white marble statues, the high ceiling with its wreathed patterns of flourishes and flowers. 'Such elegant decor!'

I smiled, taking her hand in mine, and curtseyed low, as was the fashion. 'Such a pleasure to welcome you to Kenwood, Miss Harry!'

She returned the gesture with a demure nod of the head. Lizzie, hovering behind me, grinned shyly and gave Miss Harry a friendly wave. She didn't go in for the formal introductions of the day.

Nancy, one of the maids of the house, lingered in the corner of the hall. Anxious no doubt that we had beaten her to the door, now she was waiting to take Miss Harry's cloak.

I shook my head briefly; she slipped away, understanding my meaning.

'Please, allow me!' I said, reaching up to remove Miss Harry's cloak from her shoulders. Her hair was a bright cloud of spun gold, swept up into a loosely tied crown of tiny coils. The dress she wore, tight at the waist, was full-skirted, in lavender and mauve stripes.

'And let me take your bag!' chimed in Lizzie brightly, stepping forward to take Miss Harry's equipment.

Miss Harry offered each of us an arm. 'Right, ladies,' she said briskly. 'Ready to have your image preserved for posterity?'

And with that, the three of us marched into the library, where the painting of the portrait was to take place.

Each day for a week, the Sanchos and the Mansfields gathered around a small piano in the library for our sittings. There, dressed in our finest and bathed in the sunlight ushered in by the high, arched windows, we posed for Miss Harry.

Mr Sancho and Uncle William discussed the legal cases together. Aunt Betty and Mrs Sancho planned the families' next outings to the theatre. Lizzie's sister Mary, a quietly spoken but musically gifted young woman, entertained us all with her latest piano compositions, and Frances reminded us drily throughout that we were supposed to be keeping perfectly still for Miss Harry and therefore not talking at all!

Meanwhile the effervescent Kitty, at five the youngest of the girls, held toddler Billy in her lap and together they wriggled and giggled to their hearts' content.

Throughout the process, Miss Harry directed her sitters with authority and ease. She eyed us intently, occasionally stepping out from behind her easel to rearrange the folds of a dress, or adjust the turn of a head.

I remember thinking at the time that it was one of the happiest weeks of my life. As well as being a record of the friendship between myself and Lizzie, this portrait confirmed me once and for all as a member of the Mansfield family.

Standing there at the centre of everything, I felt as though I really belonged.

So we spent our mornings for a full week, until, finally, the Mansfield-Sancho Portrait was complete.

Chapter Two

The portrait was to be unveiled at a grand Masquerade Ball at Kenwood House. Aunt Betty and Uncle William had spared no expense. Our house and grounds had been transformed into a magical moonlit Venetian garden for the occasion and over a hundred guests had been invited!

Rainbows of lanterns shimmered in the dark trees, illuminating the flashing shapes of revellers as they flitted in and out of the shadows in their costume finery. The sounds of careless chatter and bright laughter floated up from the lake where painted gondolas drifted across the water. Footmen in gold frockcoats glided among the guests with trays of bonbons, gourmandises and sparkling drinks: all supplied by 'Sancho the Grocer – Purveyor of Fine Fayre'.

In the Great Library, the portrait hung on the back wall behind an emerald velvet curtain, like a well-kept secret.

Uncle had even hired four members of the Bow Street Runners – London's emerging law enforcement agency – to guard the precious painting. Constable Meecham, a burly man with generous whiskers, and his assistant, Officer Higson, a young nervy red-headed man, stalked the Great Hall, hands clasped behind their backs, scrutinising the guests as they arrived.

I paced up and the down by the front door, impatient to see Lizzie. At last, the Sanchos arrived, dressed in matching outfits, as a pride of lions.

'Belle!' Lizzie threw her arms around me in a tight, rapturous hug and spun me about to look at my costume: a scarlet firebird, with a tall orange plume rising from my hair. Lizzie was decked out in a gold waistcoat and breeches, her dark eyes dancing with pleasure behind a mask of flaming mane and feline mischief.

'Do you know all these people?' Lizzie asked, gazing around at the gowned guests strutting like peacocks, chattering brightly, fluttering fans.

'Some,' I said, threading my arm through hers, watching the guests float into the library. Together we made our way through the crowd milling around the hall. 'Over there, the large man in the rather sombre brown coat is Dr Johnson, who wrote the dictionary! And that young woman there, in the purple and gold dress, is Frances Burney, the writer!'

I scanned the rest of the room. 'I wonder if Miss Harry is here yet . . .'

'There!' said Lizzie, nodding towards the young artist, effortlessly elegant in a short-sleeved turquoise gown, her hair twisted into a golden chignon graced with a peacock feather.

Miss Harry wore long white gloves that reached up past her elbows and contrasted with the pale honey of her skin. She was nodding demurely, smiling a little, sipping from a long-stemmed glass of champagne and deep in conversation with a tall young gentleman in a sky-blue frockcoat.

We wove our way to the front of the crowd.

'Who's she talking to?' Lizzie whispered.

I had not seen the young man before. His blond hair was pressed into curls that clung close to his head, and his attention seemed to be fixed entirely on Jane Harry. Her eyes, however, flitted around the room as he spoke, as though searching for someone else to converse with.

Lizzie nudged me. 'Look at your uncle! He's dressed as a highwayman!'

I stifled a giggle as Uncle entered the room with Lizzie's father, regal as the king of his pride. Uncle wore the black cloak, mask and tricorne hat of a notorious roadside robber. He had his arm around Mr Sancho's shoulder. Probably discussing their speeches to introduce the portrait, I noted. Mr Sancho, a great golden mane framing his face, surveyed the room surreptitiously over the top of his champagne glass.

'And Mr Gainsborough? Has he arrived yet?' he asked, nonchalantly.

I glanced around the room to see if I could spot the celebrity artist. Mr Gainsborough was currently the most renowned portrait painter of our time. According to Aunt Betty, since he and his family had moved to London, they had been inundated with social invitations.

'Ah!' Uncle threw up his arms in that way he had when something was beyond his control. 'Sadly he has sent his sincere apologies. It seems that he and his nephew are otherwise engaged this evening.'

Disappointing!

Mr Sancho's face fell. 'I had rather hoped . . . what with . . . oh well, never mind!'

'Mr Gainsborough painted Ignatius's portrait a few years back,' explained Mrs Sancho, appearing at Mr Sancho's side and patting his arm affectionately.

'And it is our pride and joy!' he affirmed roundly, adding, with a wink, 'After our own children of course!'

Mr Sancho grabbed Lizzie in a swift sideways hug that sent her mask askew.

'Papa!' she cried, wriggling out of his arms and straightening her costume.

Shot through with a sudden flash of yearning, I cast my eyes to the portrait of my own father hanging above the fireplace. How often did he think of me from across the sea?

'Girls, allow me to introduce you to Mr James Knight!' Aunt Betty, suddenly between us, started steering us towards the young man talking to Miss Harry. 'He's the son of an old family friend.' She beamed as Mr Knight turned towards us. 'And he's a student of law!'

Mr Knight bowed low. 'Charmed, I'm sure.'

I curtsied and held out my hand for him to shake. He did so firmly, with confidence. I watched him as he greeted each of us in turn. His manners were impeccable, his movements graceful. He seemed a perfect gentleman.

Lizzie lingered on the edge of the circle, watching the slow and intricate round of introductions with barely concealed disdain. As Mr Knight disappeared into another low bow between us, she raised her eyebrows at me in disbelief. I curbed a smile. I could not be caught laughing at the guests.

Aunt Betty turned to Mr Knight. 'It's wonderful to welcome you back to Kenwood!' she said, laying her hand on his arm. 'Though I must say I would hardly have recognised you! How you have changed since you were a boy!'

He gave an easy laugh. 'Well, I should hope so, Your Ladyship! How old was I when we last met?'

'I think you can't have been more than four years old!'

Aunt said, clearly delighted to be in his company again. 'Mr Knight starts work with us tomorrow, as a clerk of Lord Mansfield's,' she explained to the group. 'William's been so very busy with all the runaway cases that have been building up since the Somerset ruling. Mr Knight will be helping him with the mountain of paperwork!'

'That's reassuring to hear!' said Mrs Sancho. 'The freedom seekers could do with the support of the law right now.'

Five years back, Uncle had passed a law called the Somerset ruling. James Somerset was an African man who had escaped his so-called master, Charles Stuart, while here in England. When Stuart imprisoned Mr Somerset on a ship and threatened to send him to work on a sugar plantation in Jamaica, Somerset's friends brought the case to court. After much deliberation, Uncle ruled that Somerset should go free and that no one could be forced from England into enslavement on the sugar islands against their will. The ruling was celebrated as a victory for the enslaved. Some had called it Uncle's finest hour. It had certainly been a proud moment for our family.

Uncle moved to the front of the room and held up his hand. I shot Lizzie a look of excitement. It was time! She pushed her mask up on to the top of her head and clapped her hands together silently in front of her with a wide and joyous smile.

The music stopped and a reverential hush settled over the room.

'Ladies and gentlemen, friends and colleagues!' The warm Scottish tones of Uncle's voice rolled around the room. 'Welcome to our home!'

Beside him, Aunt Betty beamed at the crowd.

Uncle went on, his blue eyes twinkling. 'It gives me great pleasure to present this painting to you! A unique portrait of two families brought together by the friendship between our dear girls, Belle and Lizzie!'

There were murmurs of appreciation as people turned to look at us. This was the first time that Uncle had claimed me as family so publicly. I felt my cheeks reddening. Lizzie grinned bashfully and kicked my foot.

'Let this painting stand as a symbol of the friendship between our families!' Uncle raised his glass, and tugged on the cord to reveal the painting.

And there we were! Our two families, as large as life, captured on canvas!

Gasps of wonder filled the room, and then rapturous applause. Inside, I thrilled with pride. Aunt Betty and Uncle William really did love me as their own. I was part of this family, and they wanted everyone to know it!

'Ignatius,' said Uncle, waving Lizzie's father over. 'Some words from you?'

Lizzie squeezed my hand tightly.

Ignatius Sancho beamed with pleasure. 'I echo your words, sir! And will add that we are honoured to feature in Miss Harry's work. Look there – a vision of Africans and Europeans in unity! Tonight we celebrate our shared humanity! We have cast off the bonds of servitude in favour of the bonds of family and friendship. The Somerset ruling is just one step towards the freedom that so many still seek. This painting is a fitting homage to our friendship, our freedom and our future!'

He raised his glass to the guests.

'To friendship and freedom!' he declared.

'To friendship and freedom!' the crowd returned.

Mrs Sancho stepped forward and whispered into Mr Sancho's ear.

'Of course!' Mr Sancho exclaimed. 'Let us not forget the young lady, without whom this portrait would not exist – Miss Jane Harry!'

Miss Harry turned to the crowd with a bewitching smile. 'My thanks to Mr and Mrs Sancho, and to our generous hosts, Lord and Lady Mansfield. What a joy to paint a portrait that honours all its subjects equally!' she said, beaming. 'This is my wish for my work. To demonstrate that Africans and Europeans are equal in status, alike in dignity.'

'Hear, hear!' someone shouted from the back of the room.

'And,' she added with a coy smile, 'Sir Joshua Reynolds, who could not be here with us tonight, informs me that the Mansfield-Sancho Portrait is to go on display in the Grand Exhibition at the Royal Academy next month!' A ripple of admiration moved around the room. Miss Harry clasped her hands in front of her. 'I am thrilled to announce that all the paintings shown there will be judged for the prestigious Portrait Prize!'

At this, another round of applause.

I threw my arms around Lizzie in a rapturous hug. I had been reading about plans for the Grand Exhibition in *Portraits and People*! Hundreds of people would see our beautiful portrait at it! And if Miss Harry won the prize, her career would be set for life!

Uncle shook Mr Sancho's hand, pumping it vigorously up and down. Mrs Sancho and Aunt Betty each took Jane Harry by the hand, offering up their personal congratulations. Frances lifted Billy, giggling, into the air, then popped him on to her hip and drew Kitty to her side. Joshua, our family coachman and Frances's gentleman friend, watched us from the corner of the room with a bemused smile.

Let us note this moment of celebration.

Let us observe it, savour it, appreciate it.

For of course, as you will have gathered by now, it was not to last.

Chapter Three

So this is how I remember the events that followed.

It must have been eight o'clock when Lizzie and I ventured up to the viewpoint to gaze over London from the crest of the hill on the east side of the house. I remember distinctly because we heard St Joseph's bell strike eight after the speeches. There, we had exchanged gifts: outward signs of our blossoming friendship. Lizzie had given me an exquisite white handkerchief, embroidered with quill pens – in honour of my obsessive note-taking – and edged with a motif of golden bells to signify my name. I had presented Lizzie with a set of calling cards embossed in gold to celebrate our new working partnership.

Lizzie AND Belle

Agents of History, Partners in Mystery
Sisters in solving crime

Enquire at Sancho's Tea Shop, Westminster, or
post enquiries to Kenwood House,
Hampstead Heath, London

From there, we had strolled back down the hill, past the library on our right, through the orangerie, the glass-walled greenhouse on the west side of the house, into the drawing room, where the guests whirled and whooped their way through a superfast jig.

At this point the carriage clock on the mantelpiece showed three minutes past nine.

'I told you there'd be dancing!' I cried, pulling Lizzie into the circle of people galloping around the room to the exuberant music, hands joined in a mirthful merry-go-round of abandon.

Giggling and giddy we spun, faster and faster.

And then – an explosion of smashing glass stopped us all dead.

The music scraped into sudden silence. The dancers stumbled clumsily to a halt.

Eyes darted warily around the room.

'What was that?' Lizzie whispered.

Shock stopped my voice in my throat.

Shouts from outside.

'Stop! Thief! After them!'

A high-pitched scream followed. Then another, until a rising chorus of shrieks and hollers erupted and everyone was running for the doors, tumbling over each other in a desperate attempt to escape – or to witness – whatever trouble was unfolding in our midst.

'What happened? Did anyone see anything?' I asked as we spilled out of the orangerie.

'It's our portrait!' Frances cried, racing towards us out of the darkness. 'It's been stolen!'

We hurried up the path towards the library amid the chaos and the panic and the noise. As we ran I became aware of something crunching beneath my shoes. All around us, splinters of shattered glass glinted on the pathway! One of the library windows had been smashed from its frame, leaving a gaping hole like an open mouth, edged with jagged glass. Through the window, the emerald curtains on the back wall framed only an empty space.

Our beautiful precious painting, the Mansfield-Sancho Portrait, the sign to the world of our blossoming friendship, was gone!

Chapter Four

At Uncle's request, the two families gathered in the library with Miss Harry and Constable Meecham to try and ascertain what had happened, while the rest of Meecham's officers questioned the guests in the orangerie.

Mrs Sancho stood by the fireplace, her arm around Jane Harry's shoulder as the artist stared in disbelief at the bare wall. Mr Sancho held Mary and Kitty to his side, making reassuring shushing noises to quiet their crying. Aunt Betty sat on the sofa, her cheeks pale with shock, Billy on her lap. Frances and Joshua whispered urgently to each other in the corner of the room.

Lizzie was curled up in an armchair, her knees pulled tightly to her chest. She had torn off her mask and it lay on the floor beside her. She stared silently into the fire that jumped and crackled in the hearth, her brow a tangle of fury.

I squeezed into the chair next to Lizzie and draped an arm around her shoulder.

It seemed so unjust! One minute we had been celebrating such a joyous occasion, and now, here we were, shocked, confused and at a loss as to what had just happened.

Who would want to do a thing like that?' Lizzie said under her breath, still staring into the flames. 'That's a picture of us! It belongs to us!'

She was right. It felt odd, the thought that someone out there, someone unknown to us, had in their possession this precious picture of us and our families.

'What could anyone want with it?' I wondered aloud.

Hands clasped, we sat, pressed side by side, and prepared ourselves to listen with full attention.

'So, Meecham, please tell us exactly what has happened here,' said Uncle, his voice slicing razor-sharp through an atmosphere tight with tension. I drummed my fingers on my lap, longing for my writing materials, desperate to take notes; for now I would have to commit the conversation to memory.

Meecham drew himself up to his full height. 'I stood guard at the library door just as you asked, sir! Two of my officers were stationed at the front door and another was guarding the stairs to the upper floors.'

He paused, rearranged his shoulders. All eyes were fixed on him.

'At eight o'clock I locked the library door and evacuated the hall so that no one would have access to the library while the portrait was in there, sir.' He tugged at his collar. 'But as you can see –' this addressed to the rest of us – 'the thief – or thieves – entered the library via the window from the gardens.'

Instinctively we all turned to look out of the window.

So someone – the thief – had been among us at the party then?

Meecham turned back to Uncle. 'Quick as a flash he must have been, sir. I heard the smash, and made to enter quick sharp! But the key jammed in the lock. I daresay they'd blocked it with something! By the time I got into the room, both the blaggards and the portrait were gone!'

'Confound it, Meecham!' Uncle's eyes blazed with fury. 'I hired you specifically to provide us with watertight security on the night, man! Your job – your only job, I might add – was to protect my grounds and property! And now the painting's gone! How do you explain that?'

Lizzie and I shared a glare. No wonder Uncle was so angry with Meecham and his men. They had not exactly demonstrated lightning responses.

'I did my best, sir, but they'd clearly planned it in advance!' Meecham protested.

'So there were two of them?'

Meecham swallowed. 'Yes, sir. I believe so, sir.'

'And that was it?' Uncle persisted. 'You didn't give chase?'

Meecham looked offended. 'On the contrary, sir, I jumped out of the window and chased after them up the east slope. But I lost them on the far field. It was dark, and they disappeared into the woods on the north-east edge of the Heath.' He shook his head in disapproval. 'I can only assume they had a coach waiting.'

A young red-headed Bow Street Runner popped his head around the door. 'Er, there's a witness here I think you should speak to, sir.'

'Thank you, Higson!' said Meecham. 'Show him in!'

Higson ushered in the young man in the sky-blue frockcoat, who stepped forward, taking in the room.

'James Knight, sir, at your service,' he said, with a click of his heels and a low bow.

'A bit over the top, no?' whispered Lizzie. I glanced towards Aunt Betty, whose eyes were fixed on Mr Knight.

Uncle shook Mr Knight's hand and waved him into the room. 'What did you see, James?'

'Well, I'm not much of a dancer,' Mr Knight said with a nervous laugh, 'so I was walking outside on the slopes when I heard the window smash.'

He paused.

'Go on, please, Mr Knight,' said Aunt Betty.

Mr Knight cleared his throat. 'Of course, the noise attracted my attention,' he said. 'So I made my way towards the house. But then I saw shapes in the darkness, moving up the hill towards the stables.'

Aunt Betty leaned forward, her handkerchief held to her chest. 'Did you see their face?'

Mr Knight shook his head. 'At the time I had no idea there had been a theft. Now of course I realise that it could have been the thieves I saw. And then Constable Meecham came flying past me. I followed, but . . . we lost them on the far field.'

I raised my eyebrows at Lizzie. Knight's account tallied with Meecham's, at least.

'Thank you Mr Knight,' said Aunt Betty, wearily. 'You've been very helpful.'

'Well, I'm staying at the Spaniards Inn if you need to speak to me again.' This was addressed to Meecham. Turning back to Uncle, he added, 'And I look forward to seeing you tomorrow, sir.' He thrust out his hand.

'Thank you, James, yes indeed.' Uncle grasped Mr Knight's hand in his, shook it hard. 'Tomorrow it is.'

So that was it then. Someone had broken into our house in full view of the Bow Street Runners and dozens of guests and had stolen our precious portrait! It barely made sense. How on earth could they have got away with it in front of so many people?

Aunt Betty ushered everyone out into the hall, where footmen were helping the last of the guests into their coats and cloaks. Outside, the final few carriages drew up to the door to take people home.

From the corner of the hall Lizzie and I watched as Aunt Betty and Uncle William bade their guests goodbye.

'What do you think?' I whispered to Lizzie.

'I can't believe it! Our portrait, Belle!' Lizzie crossed her arms. 'How did the thieves pull off so blatant a robbery? Sounds like Meecham's men aren't exactly a force to be reckoned with!'

'Anyone could have broken into the grounds tonight!' I said, casting my eyes up the corridor and to the staircase that led to the bedrooms. I shuddered involuntarily.

'I'm not holding out any hope for progress from them,' Lizzie said, with a toss of the head towards two of the Bow Street Runners as they collected hats and wigs from the footmen. 'We need to get to work!'

Miss Harry emerged from the library, and a footman draped a black velvet cloak over her shoulders. We followed her out to the porch where her carriage was waiting.

'Well, girls, I just don't know what to say,' she said, placing a hand beneath her throat. 'You shone on that canvas, you know. Two young women at the centre of a portrait. I've never been prouder of a piece of work.' She took a deep breath. 'It's a dreadful turn of events. I'm so sorry!'

Lizzie nodded at me. It was time to let Miss Harry know our intentions. I glanced over my shoulder to make sure we were alone, reached into the pocket of my dress and drew out one of our calling cards. Our names gleamed under the golden beam of the lamplight. I pressed the small card into Miss Harry's hand and sealed her fingers over it. 'We believe we can help, Miss Harry.'

The artist startled slightly at the gravity in my tone. She opened her hand and read the card, then looked up in surprise. 'I see!'

'We'd like to talk to you about who might have done this and why,' I explained. 'Something doesn't feel right.'

'Where can we find you tomorrow?' asked Lizzie.

Miss Harry took each of us by the elbow and drew us out of the porch's lamplight. 'I'll be at my studio,' she said. 'I rent a room at Sir Joshua Reynolds' house at Leicester Fields. I have some preliminary sketches that may help me to reconstruct the portrait. I'd like to start work on it straight away, so I'll be there from early morning.'

She hesitated. 'Come at midday. I believe there may be more to this than meets the eye.' Then she dropped her voice to a whisper. 'I think I have information that may shed some light, but I didn't want to . . .' She glanced back towards the library.

Lizzie shot me a quizzical look, then nodded at Miss Harry. 'Understood. We'll see you tomorrow at midday.'

We watched as Miss Harry climbed into her carriage. She waved a gloved hand out of the window and tapped on the roof. The driver snapped the reins, the horses pulled into action and the carriage swung away from the driveway and disappeared down the hill into the night.

The footmen were extinguishing the last lanterns in the trees, and inside the house, the servants were clearing up the plates and glasses, moving chairs back to their original places. The musicians were packing their instruments away. Aunt and Uncle walked Mr and Mrs Sancho through the hall, while the children helped each other on with their cloaks.

Joshua stopped on his way past us. In his silver frockcoat, his jet-black hair shining with pomade, he looked dashing. I had known Joshua all my life as he had been our carriage driver for many years. And though I was a 'young lady' of the house, we had begun to enjoy a friendship built on trust and mutual respect.

During our last case, Lizzie and I had discovered that Joshua was a long-time member of the Sons and Daughters of Africa. Having driven my family around London for many years, he knew every road, every street, every alleyway of the city. Now he was helping African people newly arrived to Britain from the Caribbean to settle into life in London, studying the law with Uncle's help so that he could advise them on how to protect themselves.

'I'm very sorry about what happened to your portrait, girls,' he said, shaking his head. 'A special painting like that deserve to be seen. Black family alongside white. African girls at the centre of the canvas. Something special for sure. But plenty people out there not ready yet for that kind of vision.'

He tipped his hat. 'Just something to think about.'

He held out his arm, with a sad smile Frances took it, and out they went together to ready the carriage for the Sancho family.

'Come here in the morning if you can,' I urged Lizzie as we hugged goodbye. 'Before we go to Miss Harry's. We'll get our own thoughts together first and start up a case file.'

It was *our* portrait. We clearly needed to be the ones to find it.

Chapter Five

Needless to say, I barely slept that night.

Downstairs, the wind howled through the smashed library window, a ghostly, ghoulish sound that tormented me and kept me from rest. It was no source of comfort to know that Meecham had left an officer on guard outside.

Lizzie and I had already had some experience of the Bow Street Runners. Lizzie's friend Mercury, a newspaper delivery boy, had been missing for weeks, sold at auction as though he were mere property. This was the painful prospect that still stalked our people. The slave trade haunted our ports and, in spite of Uncle's now-famous Somerset ruling, people of African descent were still at constant risk of being snatched and shipped out to the Caribbean to work in enslavement.

In the course of discovering a ring of traders in the

enslaved, Lizzie and I had unearthed countless documents revealing the sale of young people to wealthy families in country houses around England. Bills of sale for girls, boys, women, men. People's family members and loved ones sold like furniture.

Among them, Mercury.

My stomach turned over again at the memory of reading those papers.

We had passed on everything we had found to Uncle William, and Uncle had passed on the information to Constable Meecham of the Bow Street Runners. After all, they were responsible for keeping everyone safe on the streets. But Meecham had said that as those people had been bought in England and kept in England, no law had been broken.

And so they had done nothing to find him.

Slavery was still legal on our shores.

Spurred into action by her love for a friend she thought of as a brother, Lizzie had taken matters into her own hands. We had printed a hundred 'Mercury is missing' posters and had spent days going about the city, posting pictures of Mercury to walls and doors, handing them out in the streets, pleading with people to come to Sancho's with any news of his whereabouts.

But Mercury was still missing.

Now the Sons and Daughters of Africa were our best hope for finding him. Lizzie and I had discovered them when we stumbled upon one of their meetings at the Guinea Coffee House during our last investigation. Freedom fighters committed to the total emancipation of people of African descent. Men and women working together to fight slavery and all the ills it had created.

A sharp creak broke the flow of my thoughts.

It came from below my bedroom.

Was someone moving around downstairs?

I slid out of bed, pulled on my night coat and lit a taper.

Out in the corridor, there was no light coming from Uncle William and Aunt Betty's room. I peered down into the darkness of the hall.

Another creak.

It was coming from the library!

I padded down the stairs into the quiet gloom of the hallway.

The portraits that hung on the walls glared down at me in the half-darkness; my flickering taper casting dancing lights and shadows on the pale faces that eyed me as I moved through the house.

I placed my ear to the door.

Quiet footsteps, the opening of a drawer, the rustling of paper.

My heart thrummed harder in my chest. I took a breath and turned the doorknob, slowly opened the door. Light spilled across the room. A tall figure was hunched over Uncle's writing desk, reading a letter in the sputtering candlelight.

As I stepped in, the man spun around and threw his arm up over his face as though to shield himself from view. The candle toppled from the desk on to the carpet. The man leaped to stamp out the flame, throwing himself into darkness.

On weak legs I stepped forward and with a violently trembling hand I held up my own flickering light to illuminate the intruder.

It was Uncle William.

Chapter Six

'Belle! You made me jump!' Uncle William dropped the letter he had been reading; it drifted to the floor between us. He snatched it up, turned and shut it away in his desk drawer with a decisive turn of the key in the lock.

'I'm sorry, Uncle . . .'

Whatever he had been reading, my interruption had clearly rattled him. He moved towards the armchair by the fireplace and sank into it, breathing heavily.

'I couldn't sleep,' I said gently, setting my taper down on his desk. I knelt beside him and took his hand. It was cool to the touch, the skin papery and dry. Uncle was not frail, but he had now passed his seventieth year, and his hands were those of an old man.

He squeezed my hand in return with a soft smile. 'No, Belle, nor I. It has been a most taxing day.'

We both glanced towards the library window, covered by the crimson curtain. I shivered. Outside, the steady, pacing footsteps of one of Meecham's men, left behind to stand on guard.

'I have always thought of this house as the safest of places, Belle.' Uncle's voice was grave and low. 'High on a hill, a haven of peace, a place to rest, to think. I never imagined that anyone would intrude on our peace in this way . . .'

I felt the same. The violence of the theft had shocked us all. 'Why do you think someone may have done this, Uncle?'

He sighed. 'Who can say for certain, Belle? The painting could fetch a high price. Portraits of well-known people can be worth a great deal of money.'

Was this how people thought about paintings? As expensive objects? 'But it's worth more to us!' I said, searching his face for reassurance. 'Far more than any price anyone could set on it.'

He sighed, his face softened into a sad smile. 'True, my dear, and wise words, as always.' He leaned forward now with an earnest look, grasped both my hands. 'But we ourselves are safe, unharmed,' he said. 'And that is a blessing not to be ignored.'

Deep down I knew he was right. No one had been hurt

when the portrait had been taken. But the broken window, the screams of the crowd, the violent disruption of our celebration – all had jangled my nerves.

He kept tight hold of my hands as he spoke. 'A painting, a book, a piece of furniture, a house – these are all mere trifles compared to the ones we love. You, Belle, are the most precious thing in this house to us!'

He pulled me to him in a hug. My head against his chest, I wondered what had upset him so. Though we were close, Uncle William rarely shared his feelings openly with me this way.

He drew away from me and glanced up to the portrait of my father that hung above the fireplace. Papa wore the dark blue coat of his naval uniform, a white cravat around his neck. His face was pale, his eyes dark and serious. To his chest he clutched a telescope, and behind him the roped riggings of a ship were visible. That was my father. Always in search of somewhere else to be.

Aunt Betty often said that I had my father's nose and my mother's eyes. My memories of my mother's eyes were becoming more distant with each day that passed. I had to take Aunt Betty's word for it.

The sight of my mother bringing me to Kenwood on a chill November morning flashed in my mind. How tightly I had clutched her hand as she walked me up the wide road to the creamy-white mansion, huge and imposing against the cold blue sky. I had my good dress on, the purple one with the lace trim, and a brown calico wrapped in a cloth bundle at my side. Kneeling in front of me she had gathered me up into her arms.

'Write to me!' she had whispered into my hair, clutching me close.

Then without warning she was striding up the long path away from me, her braided hair swinging down her back like thick ropes, her green cloak billowing out behind her like a sail.

Such was the memory that tugged at my sleep each night.

Now, as Uncle contemplated his nephew's image on the wall, I summoned up the courage to put the question again.

'Why have I not seen my mother or my father in so long, Uncle?' I said, watching his face closely for a response. 'Why do they not visit?'

Despite the strain of longing in my voice, Uncle's face seemed to close before me. 'These matters are not to be discussed with someone of your tender years, Belle.' He looked away, towards the window. 'There will be a time for that conversation. For now, know that you are loved. Know that you are precious to us. And be content.'

He patted my hand as though to end the matter there. A surge of frustration rose in me.

Why would Uncle not tell me about my parents? Did he have any idea of the pain that gnawed at my heart when he refused to say more? Did he not realise that I felt like a blank page in our family story? The portrait had, momentarily, filled that gap for me. Had made me feel as though I really were a part of this family. But now that was gone too. And I had been reduced once more to the riddle in the family tree.

'Come, Belle, you must return to bed!' said Uncle suddenly, pushing up on to his feet. 'I must be up early to greet Mr Knight! He will be joining me to help with my correspondence. We have some letters to work over together.'

I felt a sharp stab of envy. Since the age of eight, due to the evenness of my writing hand, Uncle regularly invited me to sit with him here in the library to help with his correspondence. I would sit at his writing desk and read his letters aloud to him as he paced the floor. He would mull over his responses while I prepared the writing materials – fresh sheets of paper, inkwell, quill pen – newly sharpened, of course – and blotting paper. When he was ready, he would dictate the replies as he paced up and down the floor; I would scribe in what he called my 'most elegant' handwriting. These were cherished moments between us: an easy peace peppered with jokes and giggles to keep the mood light.

Was our precious time together to be given up for a stranger?

Uncle picked up the candle and waved me in the direction of the door. As we left the library I glanced back towards the desk drawer where Uncle had hidden the letter he was reading when I had surprised him.

Why had the letter moved him so? And more importantly, why had he hidden it from me?

But not only had he locked the letter inside the drawer – he had removed the key.

Chapter Seven

The following morning I rose early, hoping to help Uncle set up for work before Mr Knight arrived. Perhaps I could organise his writing materials for him, prepare the desk for the day.

As I descended the staircase, I heard voices in the library. The low tones of men. I knocked and went in. Uncle was standing by the fireplace, fingers steeple-pointed upwards by his lips in concentration.

At the writing desk sat Mr Knight, in his shirtsleeves and a purple waistcoat. He wore breeches of matching purple and glinting silver buckles on his shoes. He held a quill pen – *my* quill pen! – in his hand and was clearly in the middle of writing a letter. He had, I observed, made himself very much at home.

'Good morning, Belle!' cried Uncle. 'You remember

Mr Knight, come to work with me on my legal cases!'

Mr Knight did not rise from his chair, but nodded affably. 'Miss Belle . . .' His blond curls gleamed golden around his head.

I curtsied half-heartedly, attempted a smile. 'I thought I would come early to help you with your correspondence, Uncle . . .'

'No worry, Belle!' said Uncle dismissively, striding to the window. 'Mr Knight is doing that job as we speak!'

'We thought we'd get it out of the way before we start on our work,' said Mr Knight, dipping the quill pen into the inkwell – one time too many, I noticed.

We?

'I'd very much like to help you, Uncle!' I said, taking care to keep my voice steady. 'I'll be seeing Lizzie later, so I thought that perhaps . . .'

'Do not trouble yourself, Belle, dear,' said Uncle, waving his hand in the air. 'We're quite all right here, thank you!' He turned again to the window, his back to me.

Mr Knight had his elbow on the writing desk. We never laid elbows on the writing desk. And now he had left the pen standing in the inkwell, which, as anyone knew, was extremely detrimental to the delicate nib.

'It's no trouble, Uncle!' I breezed across the room towards the desk drawer where I kept my correspondence set.

Mr Knight stood up suddenly and placed himself firmly between me and the desk. He let out a laugh of surprise, held up a hand to stop me.

'Please, Belle, I must implore you . . .' He appealed directly to Uncle. 'Might I suggest, sir, that, given the rather – delicate – nature of your current caseload, it might be best to leave the ladies to their work of the house and allow the men to proceed with the business of the day?'

'Well . . .' Uncle looked a little embarrassed. 'I must say that Belle is a most insightful scribe, a superior composer of correspondence.'

Quite! Did Knight have an 'exceedingly elegant hand', I wondered?

'Of course I understand,' Knight replied, nodding sagely. 'I'm simply conscious that . . . given the rather . . . *sensitive* content of some of the most recent letters . . .'

A sudden concern clouded Uncle's face. He crossed the room and laid his hands on my shoulders. 'Please leave us for today, Belle.' He kissed the top of my head. 'I will let you know when you are next required for work . . .'

'On the other hand, if Miss Belle was keen to be of assistance . . .' said Knight.

I brightened. There was something I could do, after all!

'She could perhaps bring us a pot of tea?'

Chapter Eight

8

GROUNDBREAKING FAMILY PORTRAIT STOLEN
BOW STREET RUNNERS APPEAL TO PUBLIC

A unique family portrait has been stolen from Kenwood House in a daring smash and grab raid at the Lord Chief Justice's rural retreat.

The painting featured Lord Mansfield, his wife Lady Elizabeth, and their niece of mysterious origin, Dido Belle, pictured together for the first time since Dido joined the household as a small child. Niece Elizabeth Mary was not present for the sitting due to her current sojourn in Paris, France. Alongside the Mansfields were the family of Ignatius Sancho – known to this newspaper as 'Africanus' – composer, writer and star of David Garrick's recent production of *Othello*. The portrait was commissioned to celebrate the new friendship between the two families.

But as party guests danced the night away at the lavish Masquerade Ball, shockwaves were sent through the building as a library window was smashed and the painting was snatched.

The artist, Miss Jane Harry, a young lady of West Indian origin and a pupil of Sir Joshua Reynolds, is said to be devastated by the theft.

The portrait was due to feature in the Grand Exhibition at the Royal Academy of Artists next month. All paintings on display are to be judged for the prestigious annual Portrait Prize, worth £1000.

Constable Meecham of the Bow Street Runners said, 'We believe that the suspect or suspects may have been armed. We gave chase, but they vanished into the night, no doubt to meet with accomplices waiting with transport. If anyone thinks they may have seen anything suspicious in the Hampstead area that evening, I urge you to come forward and speak directly to me at Bow Street station.'

'Ha! I see Meecham didn't miss a chance to paint himself as the great hero!' observed Lizzie, brushing shortbread biscuit crumbs from her lap and throwing the newssheet down on the table between us. 'Don't remember anyone mentioning that the suspects were armed!'

'He certainly seems keen to give the impression that he actually cares about this crime,' I remarked.

'Makes a change! He certainly hasn't done that when it comes to finding Mercury.'

Oh, Lizzie. Mercury was still so much on her mind.

'Still no word?' I asked, already knowing the answer.

She shook her head, stared off towards the window for a moment.

Lizzie and I were sitting together at a table in the dairy, the small outhouse half a mile or so from the main house that we had claimed as our very own incident room. Here we could work undisturbed, away from Uncle William and Aunt Betty and all the servants. Now it was crammed with books, newspapers, magazines and maps, as well as a steady supply of paper, ink and quill pens, and of course tea and biscuits. All essential equipment for running an effective investigation.

Lizzie had brought the newspaper with her from Sancho's; the family tea shop was a hotbed of news, a hive of intriguing information. Sancho's bubbled from morning till night with cultural conversation, society stories and punchy politics.

Lizzie and I had got into the habit of scouring the papers for articles linked to the investigation.

For my part, I kept the dairy equipped with books from the library for extra details that might yield unexpected clues for the case. It was what Uncle called 'context'. On the table lay copies of *Art and Artists: An Introduction*; *People and Portraits: An Eighteenth Century Pastime*; *Paintings and Their Value*.

I had also sketched out a map of the ground floor of the house, showing the library and adjoining rooms, the orangerie and the gardens. I smoothed out a fresh sheet of paper, wet my quill with ink and prepared to make notes as we discussed our first findings.

'So,' said Lizzie, standing up and poring over the map. 'Meecham's theory was that the thief had got into the library from the gardens.' She traced the possible route on the map with her finger. 'From this path running along the back of the house?'

'Yes. But the usual way into the library is through this anteroom, where Meecham says he was standing guard.' I tapped on the roughly sketched doorway. 'And there are two entrances into the anteroom: one from Uncle's dressing room and one from the Great Hall.'

Lizzie considered this for a moment, her brows knotting into a small furrow at the top of her nose. 'Right,' she said. 'And most of the guests were where we were: dancing in the drawing room and parlour.'

'Which lead into Uncle's dressing room,' I added, rubbing my forehead. The fact that the crime scene was my home felt distinctly uncomfortable.

Lizzie walked to the window, tapping her chin thoughtfully. 'So if Meecham's telling the truth about guarding that door, the thief must have got in through the window like he said.'

'And Meecham said that he came into the library just as

they were jumping out of the window and that he followed them out of the window,' I said, making a note.

Lizzie spun around to face me, hands on hips. 'So why on earth did it take Meecham so long to get into the room?' she demanded. 'Surely if he heard the smash and then burst in, he should have caught them red-handed?'

She was right! I jotted down her observation, reflected on it briefly. 'He said that the key sticking in the door held him up . . .'

She shook her head. 'But for them to get into the room, remove the painting from the wall, and get out again with it . . .'

'He must have been *really* slow,' I offered.

'Or,' she said, with a note of triumph, 'not at his post as he says he was!'

I sat back to consider this. Was Meecham lying then?

'But –' she added – 'Knight's account corroborates Meecham's.'

Ha! That insufferable man! So self-satisfied, so smug, so . . .

Lizzie helped herself to a biscuit, slid one across to me. She hauled herself up on to the window-seat overlooking the field outside. We ate in silence for a moment. Then –

'What do you make of him?' asked Lizzie.

'Knight? Ugh, maddening!' I brushed my hands together

to rid them of crumbs. 'As we speak he is sitting at my writing desk, acting as though he's the head of the family!'

Lizzie's eyebrows shot up. 'Oh dear! He has rattled you, hasn't he!' She pulled her knees up to her chest. 'But I meant as a witness . . .'

I sat up a little straighter, composed myself. 'Clear and to the point,' I admitted reluctantly. Irritating as he was, I was conscious that mine was perhaps a biased view.

'He's clearly not fast on his feet, though,' Lizzie added. 'Otherwise he'd have caught our culprits!'

I twisted my quill between my thumb and forefinger and scanned my notes. 'What about motive?' I offered. 'Why would someone want to steal Miss Harry's painting? Uncle suggested money.'

'That makes sense,' agreed Lizzie. Her eyes brightened. 'Maybe it's worth a fortune!'

'Possibly,' I said, not wanting to get too carried away. 'But everyone knows it's stolen. Wouldn't that make it difficult to sell?'

Lizzie wrinkled her nose. 'Hmm, true.' Then she brightened again. 'What about the Grand Exhibition at the Royal Academy of Artists? Miss Harry said that the painting was to go on display . . .'

I picked up the newspaper and read through the story again. 'I thought so!' I said, passing it over to her. 'It says that all the paintings displayed will be entered for the coveted Portrait Prize.'

'So it's a competition!' said Lizzie, as she read. She glanced up. 'Maybe someone's trying to put Miss Harry out of the running?'

I leaned back in my chair and folded my arms, intrigued. 'Sabotage, you mean?'

She nodded. A prestigious prize, professional jealousy, the desire to win a competition above all else? It was possible!

'Congratulations, Miss Sancho!' I said, gathering up the map, the newspaper and the notes and slipping them into the leather pouch where I kept all our case records. 'I believe we have a sound line of enquiry!'

I stood up from the desk and slung the pouch over my shoulder. 'Let's see what Miss Harry has to say about it, shall we?'

NOTES on
The Case of the Purloined Portrait

- **Crime:** The theft of the Mansfield-Sancho Portrait
- **Victims:** Miss Harry (as artist), Mansfield family (as owners), both families (as sitting subjects)
- **Scene of the crime:** The Great Library at Kenwood House
- **Time and date:** July 1777 at the Masquerade Ball

Notes on the incident:
- One or two people broke into the library — from the gardens? — at Kenwood House
- Removed the portrait from the wall and left via the south-facing window on to the slopes
- Spotted by witness Mr James Knight, they took off to the east and escaped across the Heath, possibly to an accomplice waiting with transport
- Bow Street Runners failed to apprehend

Information sources so far:
- Inspector Meecham
- Mr James Knight, student of law

Possible motives:
- Money? How much might the portrait be worth? Possible sale?
- Professional jealousy? Is the thief a rival artist of Miss Jane Harry's? Portrait competition

Next steps:
- Interview Miss Harry. What else does she know?
- Establish possible rivals

Chapter Nine

Miss Jane Harry worked in a modest studio at Leicester Fields, where many of London's great artists had made their home. In fact, since the artist Mr William Hogarth had taken a studio at the sign of the Golden Head in 1733, it had become a desirable destination for painters, draughtsmen, set designers and architects.

I had read in *Portraits and People* magazine that Sir Joshua Reynolds had recently been appointed the first President of the Royal Academy of Artists. He lived in a smart townhouse on the west side of the square arranged over four floors, and it was there that Miss Harry rented a small room from which she could work.

'Right!' I said as we approached the front door, flanked on either side by tall columns. 'I'll lead the questions and take notes. You can pick up the interview if you think I've missed anything!'

Lizzie threw me a mock salute. She didn't have the same need to follow a strategy as I did and would no doubt rely on her instincts. But between us we would get the job done.

At our first knock, the door flew open. Miss Harry looked distinctly unsettled. Dressed in a brightly patterned housedress, her hair was loose, framing her face in a wide stiff golden cloud. Her face was drawn with exhaustion, her eyes ringed with dark circles of fatigue.

'Quick! Inside!' she urged, waving us in. She cast a furtive glance outside before hurriedly closing the door behind us. She embraced us both in a swift hug, then beckoned for us to follow her upstairs.

'There's something you need to see,' she said over her shoulder.

As we mounted the steps behind her, Lizzie and I exchanged a swift look of concern.

'What . . . is it . . . Miss Harry?' I asked in between breaths as we finally reached the top of the stairs.

Jane Harry opened the door on to an attic room, lit by a single shaft of sunlight from a ceiling window, and stepped back. We stopped dead in the doorway.

'Man alive!' exclaimed Lizzie.

The place was a wreck. Wooden easels lay strewn across the floor. Torn canvases had been thrown to every corner of the room. Bladders of paint had been burst open, daubing

wild splashes of blue, red, green, yellow across the entire scene. Water jars lay overturned, their spilled contents darkening the floorboards.

'What happened?' Lizzie gasped, stepping over the threshold.

I followed Lizzie inside, lifting the hem of my dress so as not to stain it with the paint that was spattered all over the floor. How foolish to have worn peach satin for our first day of investigations. Schoolgirl error.

Miss Harry stood, one hand on her hip, the other rubbing her forehead. 'I found it like this when I arrived this morning.'

First the painting, and now this! My mind whirred. Was Jane Harry being targeted?

'It must have happened during the night. While I was at the party, or later perhaps.' She threw her arms in the air and sighed. 'I didn't clear it away. I thought you should see it.'

'You were right,' said Lizzie, crouching down on her haunches to survey the wreckage at close quarters. 'It has to be seen to be believed.'

She lifted a sketch from a messy pile of torn papers that lay scattered across the floor. It was a study of her own face, sketched in charcoal from a range of angles. She cast her eyes over the other scraps of sketches strewn around the room. 'Are these all your works?'

Miss Harry nodded. 'I'd hoped to try and reproduce the portrait from my preparatory sketches, but . . . most of it has been destroyed. And,' she added, lifting a hand towards an empty bookshelf, the door hanging off its hinges, 'they've stolen all my paintbrushes and pencils. It's hard enough for women to come by such materials! If it weren't for Mr Reynolds' generosity, I wouldn't be able to do this work.'

'May I?' I asked, nodding towards the small writing desk in the corner of the room.

'Please,' said Miss Harry, waving me towards it.

I pulled a chair up and whipped out my writing materials from the pouch. I arranged them carefully on the desk while Lizzie wandered the room, sifting through Miss Harry's sketches and lifting up canvases to see what lay beneath.

'Do you have any idea who might want to do this to you?' I asked, dipping my quill in the inkwell.

'Someone who's furious about something!' said Lizzie, wiping paint from her hands with a rag and standing up.

'This is what I wanted to talk to you about,' Jane Harry said, crossing the room to a cupboard in the corner. She drew out a letter from between two books. 'I think there might be some connection with this,' she said, handing me one.

It was folded neatly into a small square, and had been sealed with a red wax circle bearing the imprint of a stag's head. The seal had been sliced open cleanly with a sharp object.

I unfolded the letter and read it aloud.

Miss Harry,

Lucky you are indeed to have secured a place in the Academy, alongside our finest artists of the age. But know that this is a place of men. A house of Masters. We are a band of brothers. There is no room for one such as yourself here. Put down your pencil and your paintbrush. Be content with your sewing box.

Know your place.

Chapter Ten

'Know your place?' My insides roiled. Such poison in these words! They dripped with contempt.

A memory flashed. Tea at Kenwood with Aunt Betty and a lady guest. The clock ticking slowly on the mantelpiece. Strained conversation punctuated by long silences. A bright laugh bubbling out of me before I could stop it, some unguarded reaction to a comment I had found amusing. The woman, suddenly ushering Aunt Betty into a corner of the room, eyeing me coldly from behind her flapping fan. I caught her comment: *'She clearly does not know her place!'*

I shook the memory away. I knew such a rebuke for what it was. A refusal to acknowledge us as equal.

'What on earth . . .?' said Lizzie, peering over my shoulder at the offending note. 'Who's it from?'

'It's not signed,' I said, passing it to her.

She read it for herself, shook her head in disbelief. 'When did you receive this, Miss Harry?' she asked.

'It was pinned to the door a few days ago. And when I arrived this morning . . .' Miss Harry flung a hopeless arm towards the mess that littered the floor.

'What a horrible letter!' said Lizzie, her lips curling in disgust. She threw it down on the writing desk. 'And what a bunch of cowards threatening a woman like that!'

A shadow seemed to pass over Jane Harry's face. She toyed with her fingernails. 'Reactions to my arrival here have been, well, varied to say the least,' she said awkwardly. 'Many of the men at the Academy don't approve of the idea of women painting. Add to that my mother's African heritage and . . . well . . .'

Lizzie flashed me a glare. Just weeks earlier, her own father Ignatius had been targeted by a man jealous of Mr Sancho's success. He had not wanted to see an African man take centre stage at the theatre. With the shadow of slavery hovering over us, our freedom to be, do, act and work as we wished was hard come by.

'Do you recognise the emblem?' I said, picking up the letter and examining the scarlet seal. It was a family crest. I had seen many such symbols on the doors of carriages that rolled guests into Kenwood, but this one was unfamiliar. 'This stag's head?'

Miss Harry frowned. 'No, I've never seen it before.'

I traced my finger over the words on the page. 'And the letter is written in a Gothic font, which suggests that the writer values tradition. But also perhaps that they want to convey an element of fear.'

'How on earth do you know that, Belle?' Lizzie asked, with a half-laugh of surprise.

'I am fond of studying script,' I said, pulling a magnifying glass out of the leather pouch. I held it over the paper to read the hand in finer detail. 'I read many of Uncle's letters for him and, well, since our last case, I've developed an interest.'

My mind slipped momentarily to the letters I had once found from my father to Uncle. I had read them avidly, greedy for information pertaining to me, or some sign as to when he might return, some news of my mother, but I had found none. I had scrutinised each stroke of his pen, every curl on every letter. Desperate for more knowledge of him, I had dedicated myself to the study of the interpretation of handwriting. Without realising it, I had learned a valuable skill for detection.

'Brilliant, Belle!' said Lizzie. 'Go on!'

'The sloping of the letters to the left suggests a reluctance to move forward, while the height of these letters here implies an untrammelled desire to dominate.' I held the letter up to the light. 'It's very expensive paper,' I confirmed. 'Even a vellum perhaps, made of calfskin. And the ink is of a rare quality.'

'It's artists' ink,' Jane Harry confirmed. She sat down in the window-seat and folded her hands in her lap.

Lizzie threw me a look. That would tie in with our current suspicion.

'We wondered, Miss Harry,' I ventured gently. 'If you might have a rival within the Academy?' I placed the letter on the desk between us. The crimson stag's head stared mutely from the folded paper, taunting us. 'The theft, this attack, these letters. Is there any chance that this is all coming from someone who might be hoping to enter the Grand Exhibition and win the Portrait Prize? Someone who would stop at nothing to protect their own chances of winning? Have any of the Academy artists given you reason to believe that they might be involved?'

Miss Harry shifted in her seat, looked down. 'I really couldn't say for certain.'

It was too late. We had seen the tell.

'Who, Miss Harry?' I prompted. 'If you have a hunch, please share it.'

Jane Harry paused, seemed to consider her options. 'Mr Gainsborough's definitely been acting strangely,' she said at last.

'Mr Gainsborough?'

Lizzie stood up straight, incredulous. No wonder. In addition to painting Mr Sancho some years back, Thomas Gainsborough had a reputation for being one of the most affable and friendly artists in town.

'Surely Mr Gainsborough can't be involved in something like this?' I said, gesturing towards the letter, the debris that littered the floor.

'I have no idea,' said Miss Harry. 'But he's been avoiding me for the past few days. Crossing the street to stay out of my way, avoiding any conversation with me.'

'He didn't come to the unveiling of the portrait, now you mention it,' said Lizzie. 'He and his nephew were invited, but "otherwise engaged" apparently. Papa was really disappointed.'

We all three looked at each other.

'Where do you think we can find Mr Gainsborough, Miss Harry?' I asked.

'At the Royal Academy, I would expect,' said Miss Harry. 'And if he's not there, he lives over at Schomberg House on Pall Mall.'

I began to pack away my case notes and Lizzie picked up the letter.

'May we take this, please?' she asked, brandishing it in the air. She went to put it in her pocket, hesitated as she found something there, pulled it out. It was one of the posters of Mercury. Lizzie held it in her hands, her eyes fixed on it for a moment, then handed it to Miss Harry.

'I wonder if you might put some of these up, Miss Harry,' she said, biting her lip. 'My friend, Mercury.'

Miss Harry took the poster from Lizzie, studied Mercury's face. 'I've seen these posters around town! Is he still not found?'

Lizzie shook her head. A muscle twitched in her cheek. 'They're still looking, though,' she said, pulling at her fingers.

I kept my eyes firmly fixed on my case notes. The truth of it was, it had been months now. Lizzie held out more hope than I did of Mercury being found.

'He's very dear to me,' Lizzie said quietly. 'He delivered newspapers to the shop and used to carry messages around the city. That's how he got his name,' she went on. 'After the Roman messenger of the gods? He knows London like the back of his hand!'

For years, Mercury and Lizzie had run around London together. After his disappearance, when Lizzie and I had walked the streets of the city, putting up posters for his rescue, she had recounted a story of their friendship for every street we walked. She told me of how they had first met while each running messages along the Strand; of how, on Hog Lane, they had fled from an angry farmer after an altercation with one of his pigs; how in St James's Park they had rescued a baby starling fallen from its nest. Mercury had sheltered the bird in his pocket for days, feeding it on crumbs of food from Sancho's before they had both released it back into the park and watched it fly off into the spring sky.

'I think of him as a brother, Belle!' she had told me, eyes alight. She would never give up hope.

Now she flicked an uneasy glance towards me. I returned what I hoped was a reassuring smile. I had never met Mercury; only knew of him what Lizzie had told me. And I felt guilty that I did not feel his loss as keenly as she did.

Lizzie heaved a sigh. 'He's being held somewhere, enslaved. No one's seen him for months. But I know he's not far away! I can just . . . I can feel it.'

She spoke with utter conviction. I only hoped she was right.

'He looks like a wonderful friend to have,' said Miss Harry, smiling at Mercury's picture. 'I'll have some copies made and pass them out, ask around.'

Lizzie smiled, but her eyes held their sadness. 'Thank you, Miss Harry.'

The artist grasped Lizzie's hand. 'I'm staying with a family in Lombard Street, near the Royal Exchange.

I'll be there if you need to speak to me again.'

'We'll keep you updated,' I assured her, slinging the pouch over my shoulder. 'But for now, let's get this mess cleaned up for you.'

And with that, the three of us set about picking up Miss Harry's equipment, the tools of her trade, and her precious artwork, from the floor.

Chapter Eleven

11

When we left the house, the stink of Leicester Fields enveloped us like a foul cloud. Here, it was said, there was a problem with the drains beneath the ground. The city's waste and sewage swirled slowly beneath the paving stones, and in the intense early afternoon heat of this sweltering day, the pestilent smells of noxious waste and rotting food wafted up through the air, smothering all.

I shook out my handkerchief and clapped it over my mouth and nose. Lizzie hid her face in the crook of her arm and we hurried south across the square, past the street artists and the singing fruit sellers, the livery stables and the horse-dealers.

As we turned into James Street, the air began to clear. I was still stinging from the words in that letter to Jane Harry. The ugliness of it, the brute force of it. And the attack on her studio. Lizzie walked in silence, hands stuffed into her pockets, eyes tracking everyone that passed us. She was brooding. Understandably. Sometimes she just needed to be left with her thoughts.

A visit to the Royal Academy might shed more light on this self-styled 'band of brothers'. If they were the thieves, they had made it very clear they did not want Miss Harry's work out there.

'So who is this band of brothers?' I wondered aloud, stepping aside to give room to a flower cart as it clattered past, pushed by a young woman, barefoot, in a ragged dress. 'And are they the same people responsible for the theft of our portrait?'

Lizzie didn't reply.

'Let's hope Mr Gainsborough can help,' I said brightly.

'If we can find him,' Lizzie muttered.

The Royal Academy was housed in a large building in the classical Palladian style at the eastern end of Pall Mall, the grand avenue where more of London's artists lived and worked alongside one another. A long, wide road lined with plane trees on either side, it commanded spectacular views of St James's Park, a perfect spot for those skilled in, or simply enamoured of, illustration.

The Academy was like a cross between an art gallery and an exclusive gentleman's club. I had been there myself on several occasions with Aunt Betty, who loved to follow the latest developments in the fashionable world of painters and their social circles. As women, we were very much in the minority in the Exhibition Rooms. Aunt insisted that that was another reason for us to keep visiting.

'Here we are!' I announced as we arrived at a double-fronted brick house with large windows along the ground floor.

I shielded my eyes to look inside. A vast hall thronged with elegantly dressed visitors. Paintings lined the walls from floor to ceiling and marble statues stood guard at intervals throughout the room.

'Just follow my lead,' I said, looping my arm through Lizzie's. I tipped my chin up, pushed open the door and in we went.

Two men stood in front of a large painting of a countryside scene, fingers to their chins, cocking their heads to the side in scrutiny. They spoke in hushed voices, in tones sombre and low.

As we crossed the room, one of the men, a small, skinny clerk dressed in black from head to toe, approached us, eyes narrowed. He had a shock of white hair and a pinched look about him, as though he had been tightly stitched into his clothes.

'Kindly state your business here!' he clipped.

I had certainly not been greeted there like that before. Aunt Betty would never have tolerated us being spoken to in such a manner.

'Good afternoon, sir!' I chimed, deciding to ignore his rudeness. 'I wonder if you could tell us where we might find Mr Gainsborough, please?'

The clerk stared us up and down before replying. I sensed Lizzie bristling beside me.

'I think you may have found yourselves in the wrong place,' he said, peering at us over his pince-nez. 'This. Is. The Royal Academy of *Artists*.'

'We are well aware of where we are, thank you!' said Lizzie, with an edge to her voice, one hand on her hip. 'We are friends – and sitters – of Miss Jane Harry.' Two men standing nearby turned and cast glances of bemused interest our way. Lizzie continued, regardless. 'She's a pupil of Sir Joshua Reynolds, who I believe is the *President* of the Academy!'

The pinched man's eyes widened with outrage. 'Yes, thank *you*!' he said sharply. 'I do not need reminding of Sir Joshua Reynolds' position here.'

I was acutely aware of the men hovering at the edges

of the room, who had now stopped their conversations to stare openly. No wonder Miss Harry preferred to work at Mr Reynolds' house.

The clerk was still glaring at Lizzie. She returned his glare without flinching.

I stepped in, my voice soft as butter. 'We would like to speak with Mr Thomas Gainsborough, please. It's a matter of pressing importance.' I was doing my best to sound like Aunt Betty.

He raised a single eyebrow. 'I'm afraid he's not here today. Indisposed. Now, if you'll excuse me, I must ask you to leave.'

I hesitated, framing my next response, when he suddenly grabbed each of us by the arm and steered us roughly across the hall.

'Hey, take your hands –' Lizzie began, but before the words of protest were even out of her mouth, he had opened the door and shoved us unceremoniously out into the street.

Chapter Twelve

12

We staggered on to the pavement, straight into the path of two women walking arm in arm, who tutted loudly as they stepped aside to avoid us.

'Out of order!' shouted Lizzie as the skinny clerk retreated into the Academy and slammed the door.

Speechless with rage, I straightened my dress with violently trembling hands, my arm smarting from where the clerk's fingertips had pressed spitefully into the flesh. In the street around us, people slowed as they passed, their eyes fixed fast on us.

Had that man really just thrown us out of the building? Shame quickened through me like wildfire. So if I visited the Academy with my aunt I could expect to be made welcome, but in her absence, my dear friend Lizzie and I were cast into the street? I made a mental note to return and let the clerk know exactly what I thought of him and his poor manners.

'We're going back in!' said Lizzie, staring hard at the door.

'What? No!' I pulled her back by her sleeve. The thought of repeating the humiliation was too much.

She spun around and held me hard by the shoulders, her face stern with resolve. 'Look, Belle, either there's something in there that they don't want us to see, or they believe that we don't belong in there.' She tipped her chin towards the Academy door. 'Either way, it means we have to go back inside!'

This was typical Lizzie. Tell her she shouldn't do something and it was like an invitation. Here we were in broad daylight, on a busy street, in one of the smartest parts of town. Right now I felt visible in a way that made me feel uncomfortable to my core. I appealed to her once more.

'But if we get caught, they'll only throw us out again, or call the Bow Street Runners!' I shuddered at the thought of Aunt and Uncle being summoned to fetch me from Bow Street station.

Lizzie snorted. 'Meecham's lot? I'm not afraid of them!' She looked up at the front of the building, taking in its three storeys, its long rows of windows. 'Come on,' she said, checking up and down the street. 'There has to be another way in.'

I resigned myself to my fate; there was clearly no stopping her. And she was right. There was bound to be a tradesmen's entrance. I waved her on and we slipped around the side of the building.

At the end of the street, two men in grey work shirts and trousers were lifting a large, rectangular package from a coach. Crouching down by the corner of the building, we watched as they shuffled along the pavement with the heavy load, then disappeared down an iron stairwell.

'They're taking the paintings underground,' I whispered, recalling my recent reading. 'Those stairs must lead to the vaults. That'll be where they keep the work when it's not on display!'

'Right!' she whispered back. 'That's our way in!'

We waited and watched as the men trudged back up the stairs and towards the coach.

'Quick!' hissed Lizzie, pulling my arm. We raced down the steps and slipped through the half-open door, pulling it closed behind us. It banged shut, sending a resounding echo through the large, cavernous room we now found ourselves in.

The vaults stretched out in front of us, disappearing at the far end into pitch darkness. The only light to see by came in diagonal beams from windows placed high in the wall at street level. Motes of dust swirled slowly in the air,

the only movement in a place as still and silent as a grave.

This was not a place to spend a night.

Our footsteps echoed on the flagstone floor.

'It feels like a church!' whispered Lizzie as we passed from one chilly chamber to the next.

The walls arched high above our heads, flanked everywhere by white pillars. The air was thick with history: each room seemed to hold memories of whispered conversations from long ago. Frozen figures carved in marble towered around us like stone ghosts, staring from their podiums with blank eyes.

Along every wall leaned large canvases draped with heavy white sheets. By my feet, peeping out of one such sheet, flowers and angels wrought in gold clustered along the bottom edge of a frame. I gently moved the sheet aside, to reveal half of the painting.

It stopped my breath with its beauty.

A young Black woman, dressed in soft white silk spotted with red flowers, held aloft a garland of roses and peonies in yellow, pink and crimson. The dark brown shades of her skin gleamed against the glowing sunset. Stormy clouds gathered and billowed behind her. Her face, round-cheeked, soft-skinned, was turned upwards with a sombre look. A necklace of pearls encircled her throat; a single pearled droplet jewel hung from her ear. Her hair – black, wavy, glossy – had been brushed into a soft bun at the nape of her neck. A few loose tresses were lifted by a breeze that seemed to sweep through the scene.

'She's beautiful,' whispered Lizzie. 'What's she looking at?'

Together we threw back the sheet to reveal a pale-skinned woman dressed in a long silver satin pearled gown. She stood tall, towering over the darker-skinned lady, looking down at her. She reached her arms up towards a bower of flowers draped over a statue, a shadowed marble bust. When the whole painting was revealed, the white lady seemed to dwarf the Black one, the rich pearl-studded satin of her dress filling the canvas with its opulence.

Seeing this young Black girl, not much older than us, pushed down into the corner of the painting gave me an odd feeling. A tightening of the stomach, like when certain guests came to the house and I was asked to dine with the servants instead of the family. The same feeling had shot through me this afternoon on reading the vile letter written to Jane Harry. *Know your place . . .*

'So who are these women?' Lizzie murmured.

I squinted at the small engraved plate at the bottom of the frame. 'It says "Lady Elizabeth Keppel".'

A pregnant silence followed.

'So who's the other woman?' Lizzie asked.

I shrugged, bemused. 'It doesn't say.'

We turned to each other – with the same thought, it seemed. What other paintings lurked behind these sheets? Was our own portrait hidden down here, perhaps?

We flung the sheet back off another.

A white woman stood tall, holding us fast with a cold, imperious gaze. She wore a voluminous gown of white lace and black silk that hung stiffly in heavy folds about her. To her right, a small Black boy, dressed smartly in scarlet, held in his arms a silver tray laden with pink roses. Seeming on the verge of stepping out of the painting, he turned back towards her, gazing up at her, his eyes tinged with a wondering sadness. Resting her hand on his shoulder, she stared out at us, ignoring his wistful look. The label read, 'Princess Henrietta of Lorraine, attended by a page'.

My skin bristled.

We moved swiftly around the room, pulling back the sheets off canvas after canvas. All were paintings just like these. A pale white person, painted whiter than white, dressed up in their finest silks and satins, standing proud at the centre of the canvas. And then, down below, off to the side or in the corner of the painting, a young Black boy or girl, dressed in opulent clothes: brightly coloured turbans and trousers, soft white shirts, golden jewellery that gleamed against the dark brown of their skin.

In every painting, the Black child was unnamed.

In every painting, they were pushed down into the corner of the picture, holding a bowl of fruit, or a tray of flowers, and looking up, always up, towards the person at the centre of the canvas, who invariably ignored them.

These paintings filled my lungs with leaden weight. Looking at them, I felt as though I too had been pinned into a corner, forced to my knees so that someone else could feel powerful.

'It's eerie,' I said, wrapping my arms around myself to counter the vault's chilly air. 'The Black people in the paintings. Why are none of them mentioned in the titles? It's as though they're there and not there at the same time.'

Lizzie didn't reply. She was staring at the portrait of Princess Henrietta and her 'page'.

I went on. 'I mean, why put the people in the paintings in the first place if you're not going to name them? And why put them down in the corner like that? Lizzie?'

Lizzie was staring fixedly at the boy in the scarlet suit holding the tray of flowers.

I followed her eyes to the boy's face. He was about seven or eight years old, perhaps. And here he was, being presented, not as someone's son, someone's child, but as though he belonged to a princess. Like a pet.

Lizzie rubbed at her eye with the heel of her hand.

And I realised, too late again, that her thoughts were with Mercury.

Chapter Thirteen

13

Suddenly, men's voices from up the corridor.

I threw the cover back over the painting and scanned the room for a way out, having abandoned all thought of finding Mr Gainsborough or our portrait. There seemed to be no exit, bar the door we had come in. Only a wooden stepladder in the corner of the room.

Footsteps echoed down the hall towards us.

I pulled at Lizzie's arm. 'Lizzie! We've got to go!' We did not want to get caught down here.

She came to suddenly, as if out of a dream, and scanned the room. 'Up there!' she said brusquely, nodding to the small window high in the wall. 'It's our only chance! Grab the ladder!'

We took hold of the ladder and dragged it over to the window. The voices fell silent at the sound.

'Who's there?' a voice barked.

'I'll climb up first, then haul you through!' Lizzie whispered.

She grabbed a plank of wood from a trestle, tucked it under one arm and began the wobbly climb up to the window. She pushed at it. It stuck fast.

The voices were nearing.

She looked down at me over her shoulder. 'Cover your face, Belle. I'm going to smash the glass.'

I held the ladder tight and turned my face away while she thrust the plank through the glass. It shattered instantly, leaving an angry pattern of jagged edges around the frame. She tapped at the shards: I heard them smash one by one on the pavement outside.

The steps moving up the corridor broke into a run. My heartbeat picked up speed.

Wrapping the sheet around her hands Lizzie gripped the empty frame and hauled herself up through the window, her small, booted feet disappearing last. After a moment her face poked back through the opening.

'We're in a back street!' she hissed. 'It's quiet enough, but you'd better hurry!'

I began climbing, but something was stuck, pulling me back: the skirt of my dress, caught on a nail on the ladder!

'Belle, quickly, or else we'll get caught!'

'I'm stuck!'

My breath came faster and faster. I yanked the satin from the nail, tearing a great hole in the hem. I hitched my skirts up and tied them into a knot between my knees, then climbed the ladder as quickly as I could. Without anyone to hold it, it wobbled precariously.

Lizzie stretched a hand towards me. I placed one foot on the top of the ladder. It leaned to the right with my weight. All my breath seemed to leave my body. I grabbed at Lizzie's hand to steady myself. The ladder was still.

'Take this!' I slipped the leather pouch from my shoulder and reached up to pass it through the window.

Lizzie strapped it over her shoulder and reached down towards me. 'Take my hand!' she said. 'Tight as you can!'

Gingerly, I placed my foot on the top rung of the ladder. Centred it. Grabbed Lizzie's left hand with my right.

'Give me the other hand too!'

My left hand was holding the window frame. If I let go even for a second, surely I would fall! My heart lurched. 'I can't . . .'

'You can! Just step up and push your weight forward. I'll pull you through.'

I swallowed hard. Somewhere behind me, keys rattling in the door, the door opening.

I stepped up again, lifted myself so that my trail foot left the ladder. As the structure beneath me pushed backwards, I threw my weight forward through the window. The ladder went crashing to the ground. Half in, half out the window, my legs scrabbled in panic against the wall.

Footsteps running towards me.

A hand swiping at my foot, grabbing my boot.

Cold terror jolted through me.

I kicked back with all my strength, yanked my foot free, pushed myself through the gaping open window and tumbled out on to the pavement, sprawling beside Lizzie on the broken glass that spangled the cobbles. Not stopping to take breath, we clambered to our feet, shook the glinting shards from our clothes and sprinted off up the street.

Chapter Fourteen

We ran and ran until we reached the far side of the park, just around the corner from Sancho's on Charles Street. Blinking in the early evening sunshine, shaken and confused, we paused by a broad oak tree to gather our thoughts and recover our breath.

My legs were trembling, my hands stinging.

Were any of those paintings entries for the Grand Exhibition? Were those the kinds of images that would be displayed and celebrated? They had left me feeling sick. Why had people like us been painted that way over and over again? Who wanted to see us like that and why?

And why had we been thrown out, chased away like that? Made to feel as though we did not belong there?

It was Lizzie I needed to worry about, though. Seeing those paintings had clearly driven Mercury's absence home even harder for her.

'Are you all right?' I asked, laying my hand on her shoulder.

'We can't go home looking like this,' she muttered, ignoring my question and indicating our clothes. 'Mama will throw a fit.'

I looked down at my dress. It was ripped through at the hem and covered in tiny fragments of glass. Lizzie's shirt was torn at the shoulder. I grabbed her hands: her palms were flecked with blood from where she had smashed the window.

'I'm fine!' she snapped, drawing back sharply and wiping her palms on her trousers. Stung, I turned away from her and carefully brushed myself down, doing my best to cover the traces of our ordeal. Lizzie shook out her arms and legs, fiddled awkwardly with the material at her shoulder. I resisted offering my help a second time.

Darkness was falling around us by the time we were making our way out of the park. It clearly wasn't the right time to ask Lizzie if I could stay on with her and her family for dinner, so I needed to get home before Aunt and Uncle started to worry. If Joshua was at Sancho's visiting Frances, perhaps I could jump in the carriage with him.

'Belle!' exclaimed Lizzie, stopping suddenly in the street. 'The vault window – when I smashed it through, the glass fell on to the pavement . . .'

'Right . . .' It was true – we had left an awful mess behind us.

'But I broke the glass from *inside* the room!'

'Yes?' I still didn't see what she was getting at.

'So last night, if the library window had been broken from the outside by the intruders, surely most of the glass would have been on the library floor?'

'But the shattered glass was on the path!' I murmured, finally getting her drift. 'So it must have been smashed –'

'From the *inside*!' she affirmed, spreading her arms wide.

It was a brilliant observation.

'But wait,' I said, walking alongside her now, relieved that her mood had improved. 'If the glass was smashed from the inside, that means that the thief was inside the house all along!'

'And means it could even have been a guest at the party,' Lizzie suggested.

I let out a sigh of exasperation. 'But the Bow Street Runners let all the guests go while we were in the library!'

'Ha!' she said sardonically. 'How typically incompetent of them!'

Those portraits we had discovered in the Academy were a significant find for the investigation, I was certain of it. It was as though they were the polar opposite of Miss Harry's portrait of our families: designed to have a completely contrary effect. Were they connected in some way to our own portrait's theft? My brain pounded with confusion. Could the Bow Street Runners potentially have let all our suspects go in one fell swoop?

Now I felt as though we had taken one step forward and two steps back.

The windows at Sancho's gleamed in the dark with a homely golden glow. Lizzie pushed open the shop door and the silver bell tinkled over the top of a bittersweet melody that ribboned towards us. As we stepped inside, the smoky scent of burning firewood enveloped us. Twisted yellow flames leaped and hissed like snakes in the fireplace.

A mournful mood hung heavy in the air.

In a corner of the room stood a young man, playing a melancholy tune on a violin. He wore a red necktie and his hair was combed out into a black halo around his head. Eyes closed, he swayed gently in time with the music, lost in its spell. A few customers sat dotted here and there at tables, nursing steaming cups of tea. They looked up with tired eyes as we entered, but no one spoke.

'Good evening, Mr Cole,' said Lizzie, nodding her head to an elderly man hunched over a bowl of soup. His eyes were colourless, his beard grizzled against his dark skin. 'Where is everyone?' she asked, looking around.

Wordlessly, he nodded towards the back of the room, where a sign announced 'Meeting in Progress'.

We wove through the tables, nodding at the silent customers as we passed, and went straight on through to the Sancho family parlour. Here the Sanchos hosted literary soirees and political gatherings. Generous and congenial hosts, they were devoted to offering up their family home for the good of the community.

The room, though small, was crammed wall to wall with people. In the front row, Frances and Joshua nodded to us as we came in. Next to them, Mr and Mrs Sancho themselves. Mrs Sancho threw us a soft, sad-eyed smile. A couple of women eyed me sharply up and down as we passed along the row behind them to two empty seats.

Something was definitely amiss.

'Welcome, Sons and Daughters of Africa! Good to see so many of you here!'

At the front of the room, addressing the gathered crowd, was Captain Meg, the Daughter of Africa responsible for the search and rescue of people enslaved or at risk of enslavement. As well as leading the rescue missions, Meg oversaw the safe houses where people could hide after they had run from their enslavers. In fact, she had rescued

Lizzie and myself from a slave trader at the docks just weeks ago – a memory that sent new shivers of dread through my body. When she saw us, she placed her fist over her chest in the Sons and Daughters sign of mutual respect and solidarity. We returned the gesture.

'So, on to our updates,' said Meg, in her gravelly drawl. A woman built for strength, her hair was cut close to her head and, like Lizzie, she wore breeches and a white shirt. She paced up and down in front of the crowd, her boots marking time on the stone floor.

'We've been making our way through the list of young Brothers and Sisters that have gone missing in the last few months,' she announced. 'We know that dozens of young people have been sold, many of them to wealthy families around England and Scotland, to work as enslaved servants in their households. As you are all aware, we passed a copy of this list to the Bow Street Runners, so that they could help us to find the lost members of our community.'

'All that evidence we gave them! And what have they been doing?' shouted a young woman in a grey dress.

'They're just sitting on it!' an older woman spat in disgust.

Lizzie raised her hand tentatively. Meg nodded for her to stand and speak.

'Is . . . is there any sign of Mercury yet?' she asked in a small voice.

There were murmurs, mutterings, whispers of sympathy.

Meg shook her head. 'I'm sorry, Lizzie. We're still looking. Many of these households have their so-called servants follow them around in the streets, in the park.' She threw her arms up. 'We've all seen them.'

'Like pets! It's disgusting!' a man in a scarlet jacket cried.

Meg continued. 'But some are keeping them hidden. No one's spotted Mercury out in the streets, or on errands to market and the like.'

Lizzie sat down, biting her lip in the way that she did when she was anxious. I covered her hand with mine; she squeezed it tight, keeping her eyes on Meg.

'The Somerset ruling was supposed to make us safe!' said a young man at the front of the room. 'But we're still disappearing from the streets!'

My cheeks grew hot. At the time, people had celebrated Uncle's ruling as though it meant the end of slavery was near. Perhaps it had not made such a difference as I had believed after all?

'This is why our own missions are so important.' Meg held up her hands to quiet the simmering crowd. 'And we have had some intelligence as to what is happening to these young people in the houses. Brother Cugoano? Please.'

Brother Cugoano was an active freedom fighter and a radical writer. A tall young man, with serious eyes, he stepped up to the front, speaking slowly, and with purpose.

'We've been informed by some of our rescued brothers that the main purpose of these recent kidnappings is for the production of power portraits,' he began.

'Power portraits?' inquired a young voice at the front of the room.

'Wealthy families are having their portraits painted to make them look as rich and as powerful as possible,' Brother Cugoano explained. 'They dress up in fine costumes and sit for the paintings in front of their land, their house, with the property on view. Having an enslaved African servant is seen as a status symbol. Paint one into your portrait to put your power on view! Show yourself as a so-called master or mistress over another human being by depicting them on their knees, or down in the corner of the canvas. While being kept as property, these young people are being painted into a permanent state of servitude.'

Lizzie threw me an anguished look. So this was what was behind the paintings we had seen in the Royal Academy vaults that afternoon. No wonder they had made us feel so uneasy.

'And we're finding that once the paintings are complete, the young brothers and sisters are sent off to the plantations.'

A sudden chill rippled through my blood. Such a fate had nearly befallen Lizzie and myself just weeks back. People as young as us were being sent off on their own to the brutality of plantation life. Plantation owners were notoriously cruel. Enslaved people working the sugar plantations faced such harsh treatment that many of them did not survive long.

'When we have served one use, we are sent off to serve another,' a voice said behind us.

'It is a shame and a disgrace!' someone shouted from the back.

Brother Cugoano nodded. 'Indeed it is.' He drew himself up to his full height, placed his fist over his chest and declared, 'We are people, not property!'

'People not property!' returned the room in unison.

'So let's get them all out of there!' cried out the woman who had spoken up first. 'What are we waiting for?'

'As you know, that is the key objective of the search and rescue missions! But resources are tight and we're acting on fragments of evidence,' said Meg. 'And now,' she sighed, 'we're running into problems at some of the houses.' She paused. 'It grieves me to announce that we have suffered yet another ambush.'

Angry cries went up around the room.

'Last night, Brothers Jonathan and Jupiter and Sister Sarah were intercepted as they approached a house in Surrey during an attempt to rescue a young brother from servitude,' Meg went on. 'They were arrested soon after and locked up at Bow Street.'

'This happened to two Sons of Africa just two weeks ago!' a woman with a high-pitched voice cried out.

'It can't be a coincidence,' said a man with a strong West African accent, shaking his head.

The room erupted once more in shouts of concern.

'Hush please, people!' said Meg, holding up a hand. The room quietened into murmurs. 'These landowners are definitely on the counterattack. We have reason to believe that there has been some breach of security. Someone appears to be feeding through information about us and our operations. When we arrive on the grounds, they are ready for us. They come out shooting and the Bow Street Runners arrive soon after.'

My head swam. So the Sons and Daughters of Africa were under attack from the Bow Street Runners? And being arrested and imprisoned! The situation was far worse than I had realised.

'How do they know we're coming?' said the young girl.

'It must be a leak!' someone suggested.

Fearful whispers passed from person to person.

'It's too soon to say,' said Meg. 'But until we know more, we must suspend all missions. It's just too risky right now. We can't suffer any more arrests.' She swapped a grave look with Brother Cugoano. 'Though it pains me to do so, I must ask you all to hold back from any rescue missions until further notice. Just wait for me to give the word, and on no account attempt any kind of rescue mission without our backup.' She looked sternly around the room. 'I hope that's clear.'

People exchanged wary glances. Where was the leak coming from? Who was sharing secret information outside the group?

A tall young man in a brown waistcoat stood up suddenly. 'What about him?' he demanded, pointing straight at Joshua, who was sitting with Frances. 'He's way too close to the establishment, man! Back and forth between the Mansfield house and the Sons and Daughters!'

My skin began to prickle with sweat. 'The Mansfield house'? Were we seen as some kind of enemy then?

Joshua was on his feet in an instant. 'You got to be joking me, man!' He turned to appeal to the room. 'You know how long I been working for this organisation? You got a worry about me, you got a worry about us all!'

The brown-waistcoated brother tipped his head dismissively towards the back of the room. 'What about the Mansfield girl there?' he said, quietly, but with force. 'You vouch for her?'

People shifted in their seats and some turned to stare at me over their shoulders. Lizzie kept a tight hold of my hand.

Mrs Sancho sprang to her feet. 'I can vouch for Belle!'

She tapped her chest vigorously with her finger. 'She as good as family to us. You got no worries from that side.' She turned and gave me a solemn nod before spinning back to face my accuser. 'So you just leave her alone now!'

'You sure about that, Ann?' said a round-faced woman from the edge of the room, inspecting her fingernails. 'I'd say two young girls running around our business pose a serious risk to security.'

Two women on either side nodded their agreement, arms folded in disapproval. Lizzie and I exchanged bewildered looks. Did people not realise we were trying to help?

'That's enough from you, Sally!' Mrs Sancho's eyes blazed. 'Weren't you fourteen years old when you ran your first mission wi' us? And may I remind you that this is MY house you in right now. My daughter's house too! This our dining room you sitting in and Lizzie made those scones you feasting on while you run her down. So if you don't like Sancho business in your business, you can take your business out in the street!'

'Hear, hear!' said the people sitting around us. Others tutted disapprovingly. There were grumblings, mumbled apologies, a shamed hush. But by now my skin was crawling with unease. After everything Lizzie and I had been through, were we still not to be trusted?

Was *I* still not to be trusted?

Flushed with shame, I pushed up on to my feet.

'Belle!' Lizzie grabbed for my hand but I shook her off, pushed my way out of the room, through the shop and out into the street.

Chapter Fifteen

Outside, the heavy heat had broken into rain, its pattering music rising as it darkened the cobblestones.

I hurried up the street, letting the rain soak through my hair, letting it cool the hot flush of humiliation in my cheeks. That the Sons and Daughters of Africa were repeatedly being caught and arrested had come as a shock. I had seen the dank cells at Bow Street once with Uncle. No one would have chosen to spend time there. How could anyone suspect me of betraying the people who were fighting for what I believed in?

'Belle!'

It was Joshua, driving the carriage slowly alongside me, the blinkered horses nodding up and down as they trotted along the cobbles.

'Get in!' he yelled above the noise of the driving rain. 'You'll catch your death!'

He stopped the carriage and jumped down. He took my arm with one hand and opened the door with the other. His kindness brought fresh tears to my eyes.

'May I ride up next to you, please?' His company would bring more solace than the roof of the carriage.

I climbed up next to him and pulled up my hood. He handed me one of the pairs of reins. We snapped them together, and the two mares, Venus and Persephone, strutted on, heads down, through the driving rain.

As we pulled out of the city up towards Hampstead, the rain eased off. Joshua clicked gently at the horses to slow them down.

'Pay no attention what you heard at the meeting,' he said gently.

I stared out over the Hampstead fields that rolled away from us to the east and the west.

'Everybody anxious right now,' Joshua went on. 'We facing tough times. We under threat. People running, people getting caught. People making accusations, laying blame cos it feels safer knowing who the enemy is.'

I looked at him now. He was not yet twenty, but he had been self-sufficient since the age of twelve, finding work with our family first as a stable boy, then a groom, until finally he had asked for – and been given – the responsibility of driving the family carriage.

A single muscle in his jaw twitched. Those harsh words at the meeting had been directed at him as well as me. And he didn't deserve them.

'I don't believe we have a leak,' he went on. 'I think we're being betrayed from outside the organisation. The people that own those huge houses are devilish protective of their land, their property. How do you think the rich stay rich?'

He flashed me a smile. I knew he was trying to make me laugh, but I still felt miserable.

'But why would the Sons and Daughters of Africa suspect me of betrayal?' I said, turning to him. 'After everything that Lizzie and I have been through, everything we've done?'

Joshua snapped on the reins. The horses gathered speed as we drew nearer to Haverstock Hill. 'There are some people that believe your uncle could have done more to protect us,' he admitted. 'Somerset's case was a real chance for us to push towards immediate Abolition. But the West India sugar merchants are still making money from slave-grown sugar. They don't want slavery outlawed. Instead they're putting pressure on your uncle to make sure things stay the way they are.'

I slumped dolefully in my seat. So this was why people viewed 'the Mansfield house' as potentially not to be trusted. Uncle had not done enough, soon enough.

We turned up Hampstead Lane and made our way down the slope that led to the house. A thought occurred to me.

'Have you told Uncle what you've told me?' I asked. 'That he could be doing more?'

Joshua kept his eyes on the road ahead. 'I have to be a little bit careful with your uncle, you know,' he said, pulling the horses to a stop. 'Can't be seen to be trying to sway him one way or the other. I was working on making sure that our people would get the legal protection they needed if they ran away from their captors.' He scratched his cheek thoughtfully. 'But your uncle got Mr Knight for that work right now.'

So he had also been ousted by Mr Knight, it seemed.

Joshua stopped the carriage outside the house. Downstairs, the lamps were still lit. Maybe I could speak with Uncle.

'Thank you, Joshua,' I said, jumping down from the perch.

He reached over to the back seat, lifted a large wooden box from the back seat.

'Here,' he said, passing it down to me. 'This won't solve anything, but it might help you feel a little bit better!'

It was heavy.

'What on earth's in it?' I asked.

'Groceries from Sancho's. Peppermint tea, plum jam and

butter biscuits. Mrs Sancho thought you could do with a little love from the Sancho family.'

Even now, even at such a time.

'Thank you,' I said again, feeling a lump come to my throat. Gratitude. 'For everything.'

He tipped his hat. 'Try not to worry, Belle,' he said. His eyes caught the ripped hem of my dress, threw me a look of warning. 'And keep yourself safe, you hear!'

And with that, he snapped on the reins and the carriage disappeared on up the lane towards Highgate.

As I entered the house, Aunt Betty was coming out of the library, looking rather austere in a dark grey dress, her face etched with worry. When she saw me she waved towards the library door in exasperation.

'Belle, your uncle is impossible at times! I've told him and told him to go to bed but he is still up working! He says he is looking for a file of important papers that have gone missing.' She wrung her hands together. 'But this morning he was complaining of palpitations!'

That sounded serious. 'Palpitations?'

She patted her chest. 'Flutters of the heart. I fear he is working too hard!' She rubbed her forehead with the back of her hand, glanced at the box I was holding. 'What have you got there?'

'Groceries from the Sanchos.'

'How very kind!' she exclaimed. 'Please pop it into the kitchen, there's a dear.' She looked back towards the library door. 'Well, see if you can persuade him to finish up and go to bed, please! You might fare better than I have.' And she kissed me briskly on the cheek and made her way upstairs to bed.

I heard voices in the library. Uncle and Mr Knight. Balancing the grocery box on my knee, I knocked. Mr Knight opened the door. Over his shoulder I could see Uncle sitting at his writing desk.

'I'm sorry, I didn't want to disturb –'

'What on earth have you got there?' Mr Knight asked, eyeing the box.

'It's groceries from Sancho's,' I said, a little louder than necessary, hoping to catch Uncle's attention. 'Treats for the family!'

Mr Knight took the box from me. He clearly expected me to leave. I wasn't going to give him the satisfaction. I thought again of the letters I had once helped Uncle to write. My eyes, still hot from before, now stung.

'Aunt Betty suggested that I try and persuade Uncle to go to bed,' I said.

Mr Knight glanced back at Uncle, who was immersed in his reading. 'It's kind of you to offer, but we're rather busy, Belle.'

Not so fast, Mr Knight. I tried again. 'She mentioned that he had lost a file of papers. Perhaps I could help find it while you two continue with your work?' Surely he couldn't object to such an offer?

Mr Knight lowered his voice. 'It's wonderful that you want to help, Belle. Really. But your uncle and I are working on some very challenging cases.' His face took on a troubled look. 'The information is sensitive, confidential. You understand – it's a matter of people's safety. I'll make sure we finish up soon and that your uncle can retire to bed in due course. And . . . thank you for the supplies! Very kind!'

And he closed the door between us.

Chapter Sixteen

16

Dear Belle,

Why did you run off like that? I've been really worrying about you!

Mama says you should ignore what some of the Sons and Daughters of Africa are saying. Everyone is frightened. More and more members of the group are being arrested – Mama says it feels as though we are truly under attack! And instead of helping us, the Bow Street Runners are the people we fear most right now.

Belle, I can't stop thinking about Mercury. Mama says I have to be patient. She says that as soon as the rescue missions are back on, Mercury is the top priority. But ever since we saw those paintings in the vaults at the Academy I've been wondering whether he is being painted into pictures that way. Knowing what we now know from Brother Cugoano and Meg about the power portraits, I am certain of it.

Write back as soon as you can,
Lizzie

Dear Lizzie,

I am so sorry to have left the way I did yesterday. I hope you can forgive my rash response.

Your family have always made me so welcome in your home. It was quite a shock to hear that some of the Sons and Daughters of Africa simply don't trust me.

I realise how upset you must be feeling about Mercury. As soon as the Sons and Daughters resume their rescue missions we can join the search for Mercury.

Uncle is working on runaway cases as we speak. Apparently they have been building up since the Somerset ruling. More and more people are hoping to find freedom by running from the houses where they are held. Mr Knight is helping him with that. Perhaps that will move things on more quickly?

I want to help too, but I am told not to 'worry myself' with such things. Uncle's definitely hiding something from me. Why do so many men seem to believe that anything important that needs doing should be done by men alone?

I will see what else I can find out about progress with the runaway cases.

Meanwhile, I've been reading about Mr Gainsborough and I enclose a clipping from a newspaper article with this letter. We need to know whether he was involved with the theft of our portrait and the threats to Miss Harry. And what does he know about the power portraits, I wonder? Any clues there might also help us to find Mercury.

Let's speak to Mr Gainsborough as soon as possible. Can you try and persuade your parents to get him to the tea shop maybe?

With my fondest regards,

Your friend always,

Belle

P.S. Many thanks to you and your family for the groceries you sent. So thoughtful and kind, even at such a difficult time.

Portraits and People

Mr Thomas Gainsborough, the Suffolk-born portrait painter, is now enjoying a sojourn at Schomberg House on Pall Mall, home of so many of our bright and brilliant artists. A member of the Royal Academy, Mr Gainsborough's work is in high demand. Commissions are coming in from all sides and he is fast becoming one of the celebrities of the day.

And celebrity is the magic word when it comes to Mr Gainsborough. As soon as he has painted someone's portrait, they find themselves catapulted into stardom!

Will Mr Gainsborough be entering a portrait for next month's Grand Exhibition? Does he hope to win the prestigious Portrait Prize and become THE portrait painter of the age? When asked about his plans for the competition, Mr Gainsborough declined to comment.

Dear Belle,

It is all arranged. Mr Gainsborough is to visit tomorrow.

Join us! You and I can question and observe him.
Two o'clock at Sancho's.

Yours, in haste,
Lizzie

That night, before I went to bed, I listened in at the library door as I passed. I knocked. Silence. I turned the door handle and peered in. There was no one in sight. I closed the door behind me and stole straight over to Uncle's desk.

What was he working on that demanded so much secrecy?

I tried the desk drawer. It was locked. On top of the desk, no papers were on view but for a newspaper. I opened it up. Nothing of interest in the news pages, but my heart skipped a beat when I saw our family name on the letters page.

Dear Sirs,

To continue with the challenge to Mansfield:

Many of us make our money through the buying and selling of sugar, grown by Africans in the West Indies. If we abolish the slave trade now, how will we fill the country's coffers? How will the sugar merchants be expected to survive, I ask you?

Are we to abide by and obey the judgments of the Lord Chief Justice, William Mansfield? Just a few years ago he ruled that no African could be forced from our land to the West Indies against their will to work the sugar. Now they all begin to believe themselves free! In increasing numbers they run from their masters, defying the law.

He even keeps an African girl in his own home. Rumour has it she is his niece! Some say that she rules over the household, such is the sway she has over her uncle. Reliable sources tell me that she comes and goes as she pleases and does not consider herself a servant of the household. Has the world gone mad? Does no one know their place any more?

HH MP, West India Lobby

Know their place?

A fire flickered through my veins. Rage. Simmering, boiling, bubbling rage that someone who was a complete stranger, should write of me and my family in this way! Who on earth did this man think he was? Was this what Uncle was trying to keep from me? Was he trying to protect me from these poisonous opinions?

These must be the people Joshua had spoken of. The men that wanted slavery to continue. The men that had taken offence at the Somerset ruling and what it meant for those of us with African blood. And this 'HH' was a Member of Parliament too.

No wonder Uncle and Mr Knight were so busy.

I folded the newspaper up again, placed it carefully on the desk, slipped out of the room and stole upstairs to bed.

Chapter Seventeen

I had to steel myself to step into Sancho's the following day at two o'clock as Lizzie had instructed. Truth be told, since my loyalty to the Sons and Daughters of Africa had been questioned, I felt uncomfortable, self-conscious. Mrs Sancho's gift of groceries was a typically kind gesture, a reminder that I was still welcome in their home, but the words of those who doubted me still haunted my thoughts.

I remembered a proverb Mrs Sancho had once shared with me and Lizzie, to warn us against indulging in gossip: *Good words are food. Bad words are poison.*

Lizzie and her sister Frances were seated at a table at the back of the room, while Mr and Mrs Sancho exchanged greetings with two men I had not seen before. One was a middling-sized man of solid stature, who had nonetheless a liveliness about him, a quickness of manner. His clear grey eyes scanned the room, seeming to capture every detail. Behind him hovered a younger man, of about twenty years of age, slender-faced, with wavy auburn hair. He cast his eyes about the place with a languid ease.

'Mr Gainsborough!' cried Mr Sancho, wringing the hand of the older gentleman up and down. 'And my dear Mr Dupont. At last, you visit!'

My interest quickened. So this was the famous artist, Mr Thomas Gainsborough. Could he really be behind the theft of Miss Harry's portrait?

'Sancho!' cried Mr Gainsborough with warmth. 'My dear fellow!'

The men embraced heartily and slapped each other on the back, drawing bemused stares from around the room.

'Allow me to introduce my nephew, Gainsborough Dupont!'

The young man bent into a low bow.

'Talented, with a wonderful eye!' Mr Gainsborough went on. 'Working as my apprentice. Definitely one to watch!'

'I have an expert teacher,' said Dupont, his voice soft and solemn.

'And may I introduce my daughter Lizzie, and our dear friend Miss Dido Belle!'

The pride in Mr Sancho's voice was a deep comfort

to me. Lizzie stood to give her usual nod and wave and I curtsied. Mr Gainsborough smiled broadly. I found myself relaxing. So far, his affable reputation seemed well-deserved.

'We have much to catch up on, Gainsborough,' said Mr Sancho, ushering us all towards a table set with tea. 'Quite a sequence of events! Girls, Mr Gainsborough is the man behind the remarkable portrait of yours truly!' He gestured at the portrait that hung on the wall above the table. 'How many men of my hue have had a singular portrait painted by an English painter, that shows such dignity, such humanity!'

The portrait was indeed rare for our time. Mr Sancho alone occupied the canvas, dressed in a scarlet waistcoat edged with gold thread and a navy coat of rich fabric. His hand was thrust inside the waistcoat in the gentlemanly manner of the age. His head was turned slightly off to the side, and his mouth seemed on the brink of smiling, but it was his eyes that truly captivated the viewer. Soft, sad, compassionate and contemplative, they seemed to hold a hundred emotions. All the chapters of Mr Sancho's life story – enslavement, education, escape and, finally, family – could be read in their depths. It was a true and living likeness. Much as Miss Harry's had been of us all. Surely these artists shared the belief that Black people deserved to be portrayed as they truly were.

That didn't mean Mr Gainsborough might not be jealous of Miss Harry's talents, though, I reminded myself. He might still know more of the portrait's theft than he was letting on. I glanced at Lizzie, who was frowning. Was she wondering the same thing?

The artist waved an arm towards his friend as he sat down. 'Those qualities, good sir, are the qualities of the subject – your fine self. All I had to do was represent them!'

'I thank you,' Mr Sancho returned in earnest, pouring tea into the fine blue china cups while Frances buttered scones and piled them on to an oval plate. She watched her father as he spoke, her eyes soft with quiet admiration. 'But I fear there are not many artists working today that share your view. Look at the power portraits with the so-called "fashion accessory" of a Black servant, for example. Painting after painting appears with a young African pinned to the bottom corner of the canvas, forced to the edge of the picture! Frozen in time as servants, enslaved! It boils my blood to think of it!'

'And what about you, Mr Gainsborough?' said Lizzie, passing him a cup of tea and eyeing him steadily. 'What do you think of such portraits?'

Her question hung in the air. My stomach tightened a notch. So Lizzie had bowled straight in! But was her question too direct to elicit an honest answer? We did not want to draw attention to our own suspicions.

Gainsborough cast his eyes down and shook his head. His voice, when it came, was thick with discomfort. 'It is a sorry state of affairs indeed. A very . . . backward practice, I would say.'

'Backward – and barbaric!' Mr Sancho added. 'But there are artists working to represent us in all our humanity! True portraits that depict us as we would be seen – free, dignified and on our feet rather than on our knees!'

'Did you hear about what happened to the portrait Miss Jane Harry painted of us with Belle's family?' asked Mrs Sancho, her voice pinched with hurt.

'A terrible business, Mrs Sancho!' Gainsborough replied. 'I was deeply saddened to hear of it.'

I flicked a glance towards Lizzie. She kept her eyes firmly fixed on Gainsborough. 'And we missed you at the unveiling of the portrait, Mr Gainsborough,' she said, pushing a cup towards Dupont. 'A shame you missed the opportunity to see it while it was still in our possession!'

Eyebrows went up all around the table. Everyone, it seemed, had caught the daring edge in Lizzie's unmistakably disrespectful tone. What was she doing? At this rate she would raise Gainsborough's suspicions and ruin any chance we might have of establishing guilt – *if* he were guilty.

'Lizzie!' said Mr Sancho, shooting her a warning look.

'Ignatius, my dear friend,' said Gainsborough, laying his hand on Mr Sancho's arm. 'It is no matter.' He turned to Lizzie. 'You are quite right, Miss Elizabeth. I was very sorry to miss the unveiling of Miss Harry's portrait. But my nephew and I had a pressing engagement from which we were, regrettably, unable to extricate ourselves.'

Now it was Dupont's turn to look uncomfortable. It made me wonder about their 'pressing engagement'. Was someone else able to vouch for their whereabouts on the night of the theft? These were the questions Lizzie and I needed to ask. But not here, and not like this.

'With apologies, please excuse us!' Gainsborough was on his feet. 'My current schedule of commissions is particularly demanding. We must be on our way.'

'But you've only just arrived!' cried Mrs Sancho in dismay. 'You've not yet even enjoyed your tea!'

Mr Gainsborough bowed low. 'And return we shall, in due course. But for now, you really must excuse us.'

I shot Lizzie a look. She returned a barely perceptible nod. Was Mr Gainsborough's sudden anxiety to leave the result of Lizzie's questions?

'Lizzie, fetch Mr Gainsborough's coat from the back room, please,' said Mrs Sancho. 'Do come back soon, Mr Gainsborough. You're missed around here!'

'We could certainly do with more of your portraits for our own community,' added Mr Sancho. 'Lizzie! Hurry up with Mr Gainsborough's coat!'

Lizzie reappeared from the parlour, holding a smart brown overcoat, and handed it to Mr Gainsborough. As he and Mr Dupont left the shop, she shot me a look and tipped her head towards the door. It was time for us to leave too.

'We'll excuse ourselves as well, if we may!' she announced, slipping a handful of the 'Mercury is missing' posters into the pouch slung over her shoulder.

Now was our chance to question Gainsborough more freely.

I waved a quick goodbye, said my thanks and followed her into the street.

Chapter Eighteen

18

Outside, Gainsborough and Dupont were just hurrying around the corner of Charles Street into Duke Street. We followed swiftly, stopped at the end of Great George Street and peered around the corner after them.

'They're going into the park,' Lizzie said, breaking into a run. 'Come on!'

Irritation flickered through me as I set off after her. Why were we always running?

In St James's Park, the men slowed their pace. They were arguing. Dupont was holding something in his hand, showing it to Gainsborough, who was trying to walk away, beckoning Dupont to follow. We hovered behind the trunk of an oak tree and watched.

Lizzie grabbed my arm so hard I gave out a sharp yelp.

'Ow! What on –'

'It's Mercury!' cried Lizzie.

'What?'

'The picture they're arguing over,' she said, not taking her eyes off the men. 'It's one of my posters of Mercury! Mr Dupont must have picked it up in the tea shop!'

Dupont was holding fast on to Mr Gainsborough's arm, entreating, demanding. What did they know about Mercury? And why was it causing such upset?

'Let's confront them!' said Lizzie, stepping forward.

'No, wait!' I said, pulling her back. 'Let's just get closer to hear their conversation.'

She shook my arm off with a sigh of frustration, but gave in. We followed Gainsborough and Dupont at a safe distance, staying close to the hedges and bushes that bordered the path. I threaded my arm through Lizzie's and silently feigned polite conversation in case they should see us.

'It's him! The boy at that house! I know it's him!' Dupont was saying. 'We have to tell the Sanchos!'

'Not yet, Dupont! I can't risk it!' Mr Gainsborough replied through gritted teeth. 'You know what he said. Not a word to anyone, if I want my family to be safe. Let us simply return there this evening as planned. He said the carriage would collect us at nine.' He looked anxiously about him and pulled his nephew by the elbow. 'Come, quickly!

We've still got materials to prepare and bags to pack. I want us to be ready when the carriage arrives.'

They left the park by the north-east exit and headed towards Pall Mall.

'They're going home, to Schomberg House,' I murmured.

Keeping our distance, we hurried after them. They turned left and disappeared into a grand-looking house, fronted with columns either side of an elegantly carved porch.

Lizzie grasped me by both arms, her eyes shining with hope. 'They know where he is, Belle! They know where Mercury is and they're going back there!'

'We don't know that for certain,' I pointed out. 'They just think they recognised him, that's all.'

The street swirled with people, walking swiftly along, faces turned to the ground, pulling their coats tighter about them, seeking out shelter as darkening clouds swelled in the late-afternoon sky. Meg's words echoed in my ears. *On no account attempt a rescue mission without our backup.*

But Lizzie's fire was lit now; she seemed hell-bent on rushing in. 'They said a carriage was coming for them at nine! That's five hours from now. We can come back here later and follow them. If we do, we'll find him, I know we will!'

Under the circumstances this was reckless in the extreme! Follow them where? 'Lizzie!' I said, more firmly this time, pulling her out of sight into an alleyway that ran along the side of the house. 'Meg said we should wait!' If she would not take my own advice, perhaps she would consider Meg's warning.

Lizzie pushed me away from her then, her eyes alight with fury. 'No!'

I stumbled back, stunned by the force in her hands and the rage in her voice.

'Maybe you don't care about what happens to Mercury!' She lifted her chin. 'Maybe he's not as important to you as your precious portrait!'

Her words hit me like hailstones. Surely she couldn't mean them. I struggled to keep the hurt out of my voice. 'Lizzie, you know that's not –'

'But I care about him!' She slapped a hand to her chest, swallowed a sob. When she spoke again her voice was level, but the fire of her anger still burned through it. 'He was my . . . friend. I saw him . . . every . . . day.' Tears welled in her eyes. She blinked them back. 'If we don't try and find him, who will? The Sons and Daughters have had their security breached! The Bow Street Runners – well, they'd probably arrest him rather than rescue him . . .'

'I-I could speak to Uncle –' I stammered, lost for any other solution.

'Ha!' She shook her head as though in amazement.

'You really think he would be of any help? We gave your uncle the evidence of all those lost brothers and sisters and what has happened since – nothing! He's done nothing, Belle!'

An image of Uncle flashed before me. Hiding that letter in a drawer, turning the key.

'He gave the evidence to Meecham!' I cried. 'And now he's working on the runaway cases as we speak. It's even making him ill!'

'What good is that to us?' Lizzie threw her arms up in frustration. 'You heard what the SDOA said! Mercury and so many others are still missing. They are being held against their will! Enslaved! Until slavery is outlawed in our country, none of us are safe!'

She jabbed a finger into my breastbone, her eyes ablaze. 'Your uncle has the power to push for that decision. What is he waiting for? Does he actually care about us really? Or does he think he's done all that is necessary? Very convenient, from his comfortable house on the hill!'

I blinked back tears, unable to speak.

Lizzie straightened up, held her head high. 'I waited before going after Mercury once before, Belle,' she said, with quiet fury. 'And he's been lost to us all for weeks. Weeks! I can't let that happen again!'

She pulled out one of the posters from the pouch slung over her shoulder and thrust it towards me. Mercury's face stared at me from the page, a faint sweet smile playing across his lips. He was just a boy. Thirteen years old. Lizzie had told me once that the artist had drawn him exactly as she remembered him. With a spark in his eye. The heat of shame stung my eyes.

'I'm coming back here at half past eight tonight, no matter what,' Lizzie announced steadily. I had never seen her look so serious. 'And when Gainsborough and Dupont leave home in that carriage, I'm going to follow them to this "house", wherever it is.'

She let her arm drop to her side, her hand still clutching the poster.

'The only question is, Belle, are you with me?'

Chapter Nineteen

I stormed home across the Heath to Kenwood, Lizzie's words ringing in my ears, her fury close at my heels like a hungry dog. As the gathering wind pushed through the long grasses, the green and yellow fields seemed to crackle with heat.

Why did Lizzie have to charge into situations like that? What if we were arrested by the Bow Street Runners? What if we were captured by slave traders once more? I had been in that situation once before and it had terrified me.

The truth was, I didn't know if I had the courage to go through it again.

But Mercury's boyish face kept appearing before my eyes. He had lost his family. Yes, he had friends, but to Lizzie he was like a brother. Lizzie was the only friend I had who inspired such a feeling in me – a sense of sisterhood, beyond friendship.

How would I feel if it were her who were missing?

As I entered the wood that bordered the family grounds, I slowed my pace, turning my attention for a moment to the gentle fluting of birds in the trees around me.

How could I have been so insensitive? Of course finding Mercury was the most important thing! If Lizzie gave up on him, maybe he would never be found. But until now I had not known how we would do so. When I thought of him, it were as if he had slipped into another life, hidden from us. And now that we had discovered a genuine chance of finding him, I had felt too afraid to take the necessary steps to save him.

Added to that, the Sons and Daughters of Africa had cast doubt in everyone's minds about my loyalty to the cause – Lizzie's included, it seemed.

Perhaps it was time to prove my loyalty.

Yes – now it was time to act!

When I arrived back at Kenwood I raced up to my room and changed into my riding clothes. I would take one of the horses from our stables, and ride back into town to meet Lizzie at Schomberg House at half past eight. There we could wait for the carriage that we believed was coming to collect Gainsborough and Dupont at nine o'clock. We would follow, on horseback, at a distance.

If the Gainsboroughs really had seen Mercury, if he

really was being held in the place that they were going to, we could bring him back with us. Not as straightforward as it sounded, of course. The Sons and Daughters of Africa had been leading missions like this for years now, but we were doing this without them. Yes, they had warned us to wait, but Lizzie was desperate to help her friend and I simply couldn't let her go alone.

I prepared one of the guest bedrooms at Kenwood for Mercury in the event of us bringing him home. He could spend the night there safely and the following morning we would take him to Sancho's and hand him over to the care of the Sons and Daughters. They would arrange shelter, food, clothing. He would be safe. He would have people around him to look after him.

I had never ridden alone into the city before, but I was an experienced rider, and keen to test out my skills on the London streets. I decided to take Venus: a calm mare, old and wise enough to know the city streets, and strong enough to gallop at a powerful pace should the situation require it.

I was hoping that it wouldn't.

At precisely half past seven, I snuck out of my room, down to the stables, and saddled up Venus for the evening's ride.

The day had grown hotter, the air thicker with each hour that passed. Dark clouds swelled and swirled in the purpling sky over the Heath. I rode Venus at a gallop all the way to Parliament Hill, then slowed on the steep slopes down to Belsize Village. Once we were on flatter ground, I cantered through the smart squares of Fitzrovia and on into the narrow roads of Soho.

Cloaked and hooded, seeing the streets from on high gave me a strange and powerful feeling of independence. As dusk settled, shops banged shut their doors, windows were shuttered against the dying light. The clatter and bustle of London's day slowed and settled into a more muted evening music.

I thought of Aunt and Uncle. I had left them a note to tell them that I would be spending the night at Lizzie's. Uncle would never have approved this particular outing. Was he aware of what people were saying about him? Did he realise how much people depended on his rulings to feel safe? Every day he shut himself away in the library and worked with Mr Knight. What was taking them so long? Aunt had mentioned a file of papers that was missing – was that what was causing the hold-up?

From Leicester Fields I turned into Pall Mall. Lined with trees and studded with twinkling gold lanterns, this street held a nocturnal magic I had never noticed before.

As I approached Schomberg House, I glimpsed a figure huddled in a doorway opposite.

I pulled Venus to a stop. The figure stepped forward from the shadows and into the light of the doorway's lantern.

Lizzie.

A surge of nerves heaved at my heart. Not knowing how she would respond to my arrival filled me with a new fear.

I swung down off Venus and led her over to where Lizzie stood, leaning on a railing, arms folded.

'You came then,' she said, as though trying not to make too much of it.

'Of course,' I said humbly. I wanted to say more, but the words jumbled up in my head.

The horse nodded her glossy brown head up and down, stamped one of her front hooves on the ground. Lizzie took a step back. Was she a little afraid, perhaps?

'It's all right, she's very gentle,' I said, stroking Venus's muzzle. 'She's strong enough to take the two of us. We'll be safe with her.'

Lizzie tentatively reached a hand up and stroked Venus's face. Venus blinked slowly, a sign of appreciation.

I smiled. 'She likes that.' Then, looking up at the house. 'Any movement yet?'

'No . . .' Lizzie passed her hand along the horse's mane wonderingly. 'I've been here since seven. Nothing yet. But

Gainsborough's on edge. He's been pacing up and down for the last half hour.' She nodded towards the window at the top of the house. A shadow passed across the dim yellow square.

Across the street, a man and a woman strolling past arm in arm glanced our way and whispered to one another.

'Let's get Venus out of sight,' I suggested, taking the reins in my hand. 'We should stay around the corner.'

'Belle, wait!' Lizzie took a deep breath. 'First, there's something you should see.'

From her jacket pocket she pulled out a letter and handed it to me. The seal was broken but I could see that it bore the imprint of the head of a stag.

A ripple of unease moved through my mind.

'The stag's head again!' I murmured, opening it up. 'Just like Miss Harry's letter! Where did you get this?'

'Gainsborough's coat.'

Was she serious? 'What?'

Lizzie suddenly looked at once sheepish and proud. 'When I went to get his coat . . .'

'So you stole it!' I cut in, feeling my anger rise all over again.

She crossed her arms impatiently. 'I thought we were supposed to be investigating! Aren't you going to see what it says?'

I cast my eyes to the letter.

Dear Mr Gainsborough,

We would like to confirm commission of the portrait as discussed.
The carriage will return for you at nine of the clock this evening.
As before, your nephew will accompany you and assist you with
the work. Only when the portrait is complete as instructed will
you be fully initiated into the Brotherhood of Masters.
You will speak of this to no one, or it will go hard with you.
Your wife and daughters clearly enjoy their daily strolls in the park.
May they continue to do so.

The Brotherhood of Masters salutes you.

Loath though I was to do so, I had to read it again to
believe the words in front of me.

'So this must be from the same men that wrote to
Miss Harry!' I said.

'Exactly!' said Lizzie triumphantly.

My mind flashed back to Jane Harry's studio: the spilled
paint, the broken easels, the slashed canvases. 'Who also
vandalised her studio!'

Lizzie hesitated. 'Yes! But what if these are the people holding Mercury, as we suspect? We have to go, whoever they are!'

My chest tightened with each new realisation of what we were getting into. 'Lizzie!' I pleaded. 'We can't follow these people on our own!'

'Here we go again!' Lizzie shook her head. 'We must and we will!'

How on earth could she have kept something so significant from me?

'Why didn't you show me the letter earlier?' I demanded. 'When you found it?'

'Because I knew that if I did, you might not come!' She rolled her eyes. 'You'd probably think it was too dangerous.'

'It *is* too dangerous!' I cried.

Behind us was the sound of horses' hooves clattering on the flagstones, iron wheels grinding on the uneven road. The carriage was coming!

Maddened though I was, there was no time to quarrel any longer. I led Venus around the corner into the alleyway that ran parallel to the east side of the house. Lizzie followed, staying low. From the corner we watched as a large black carriage, like a funeral hearse, slowed to a stop in the street. Two giant grey horses with blinkered eyes snorted and stamped, nodding and swishing their tails.

The coach windows were curtained. The driver, sat atop the carriage, wore a black tricorne hat and the cloth half-mask of a highwayman. On each coach door was painted the head of a stag.

My breath caught in my throat.

Careful not to make a sound, I climbed up on to Venus and shuffled forward so there was room for Lizzie behind me on Venus's back. I reached a hand down to help her on. She ignored me, staring instead at the waiting carriage.

'Lizzie!' I whispered urgently.

Mr Gainsborough's front door opened then, throwing orange light on to the pavement.

I held fast to the reins to keep Venus still as Gainsborough and Dupont emerged and crossed the street. The carriage door opened and a grey-gloved hand beckoned the two men inside. They climbed in and the door closed behind them.

'Lizzie!' I hissed. 'Get on, quickly!'

But instead, Lizzie darted out of the shadows into the road and crouched down behind the back wheels of the carriage. What on earth was she doing? I wanted to call out to her, but I couldn't risk it.

Venus bowed her head up and down to let me know she was ready to move. Now Lizzie was climbing up on to the back of the carriage! I watched helplessly as she tucked herself up on the small platform at the back. Surely not!

As soon as the carriage gathered any speed she would be flung into the road! I caught her eye and glared, beckoning madly for her to join me.

She stared back, determined, defiant.

'Gah!' the driver shouted at the horses and snapped the reins down hard on their haunches. The carriage swung away from the kerb and lurched into the road – taking the gloved stranger, Gainsborough, Dupont and now Lizzie, tucked up into a tiny ball, with it, deep into the soft darkness of the night.

Chapter Twenty

What had Lizzie done?

I had to think fast. Follow too closely and I would surely be seen; leave too wide a gap and I risked losing Lizzie all together. My heart kicked in my chest as I counted five seconds to give them a hundred yards or so head start. Then I flung my hood over my head, snapped on the reins and spurred Venus into action, galloping east up Pall Mall, away from the house. Avoiding the glowing spots of lamplight, I rode on, watching the carriage up ahead, a moving shadow in the darkness.

As we pushed on through the heart of London, the carriage twisted and turned through the narrow back streets of the city, clearly trying to avoid detection. The pace slowed, but the route was unfamiliar to me, and every time the carriage turned a corner, I lost sight of Lizzie for a second: the fear of losing her altogether set my pulse racing.

As twilight slipped into night, the carriage began to pull up a hill. I looked around for any indication of where we might be but saw none. The angle of the climb was so steep that Lizzie had to wrap her arms and legs tightly around the pole at the back of the coach. If she fell, I would need to be ready to pick her up before she was discovered.

I watched with my heart in my mouth. Why on earth had we quarrelled with each other at such a time? Now I could only imagine how frightened she must be, hanging on to the back of that coach. And if she were discovered, then what?

At the top of the hill we continued northwards. The buildings fell behind us in the darkness and soon we were surrounded by flat fields and rolling hills. The sounds of the countryside folded around us. Crickets chirruping in the long grasses on either side of the road; night breezes whispering among the leaves of the heavy-headed trees; the soft cooing of owls and turtle doves from nests unseen. On most nights such sounds brought comfort. But now they only signalled that we were far from home, far from safety.

As the evening settled in, cold fear crept up on me. I had no idea where we were going. How on earth would we find our way back?

Suddenly, the carriage swung off to the right and disappeared up a narrow path into a wood. I steered Venus into the trees so that I could follow more closely; unseen, unheard. From the east, gunmetal-grey clouds rolled slowly, billowing and swelling above us. We pushed on into the darkness.

Suddenly, on the horizon, a large house came into view, silhouetted against the bruised wash of sky.

It was a mansion, three storeys tall, made of dark grey stone, topped with turrets and chimneys that cast strange shapes against the thick clouds. Tall sash windows ran along the front. On the ground floor each window was dimly lit from within. On the top floor, a solitary window in the corner glowed yellow. Silhouetted there, a person, standing motionless. Was it a person? Or a statue?

The carriage stopped outside the entrance. The front of the house was covered in a dense cloud of ivy. It clung to the walls and hung down around the windows in tangled clumps like matted hair. Smoke issued from chimneys perched at intervals along the roof.

I got down from Venus and tethered her to the trunk of a tree by a running stream. There she could rest and drink until our return. Crouching close to the ground, I slipped from tree to tree towards the house, stopping just short of the wood's edge.

There was Lizzie, a tiny ball curled up on the back of the carriage, motionless.

How was she holding her nerve?

Don't move, Lizzie, said the voice in my head. *Whatever you do, don't move.*

The driver jumped down and opened the carriage door. Out climbed a man dressed from head to toe in black, save for his grey gloves. His face was masked, his head covered with a grey periwig. Tallish, of slim build. His coat, well cut. Was this the writer of Gainsborough's letter? Of Miss Harry's?

I crept a step closer for a better look.

A twig snapped underfoot.

I froze.

The man stood still, surveying the woods. My thoughts turned to silent prayers. Had he heard me moving? A large bird of prey flew out of a nearby tree. I held my breath, held my body silent and still as the bird lifted off into the sky.

The man turned back towards the house, approached the door and knocked loudly. Returning to the carriage, he opened the carriage door, and in a voice low and full of menace, ordered Gainsborough and Dupont out. Down they climbed, both blindfolded, Gainsborough with his hands raised in front of him, Dupont holding on to his uncle's shoulders.

The front door swung open to reveal a young man in a white shirt and burgundy breeches, with long, lean limbs. He held a lantern aloft: a dim yellow glow illuminated his face.

It was Mercury! He was much thinner than in the pictures I had seen, and his eyes had a sunken look, but it was him for certain. So Gainsborough and Dupont were right!

Mercury stood back as the masked man grasped Gainsborough and Dupont roughly by the elbows and ushered them into the house. No words were exchanged. The men disappeared inside. Mercury hovered at the doorway for a moment, peering out into the darkness as though hoping to find someone there, some chance of rescue perhaps. I longed to call out to him, to let him know we had come for him, but remained silent as necessary, and could only watch helplessly from the trees as he hung his head, turned back inside and closed the door behind him.

Chapter Twenty-One

Lizzie dropped silently from the back of the carriage to the ground.

'Lizzie!' I hissed. 'Over here! In the wood!'

She scampered over to me. I took her by the shoulders: she was shaking violently.

'What were you thinking!' I said, torn between relief that she was well and vexation that she should have taken such a risk.

She pulled me to her in a hug then. I could feel her heart knocking through her shirt. 'I'm so glad you came!' she said in a muffled voice, her face pressed into my neck.

I took a deep breath. 'I'm so sorry, Lizzie . . .' More than she would know. More than I could even express.

She squeezed my hands. 'Me too, Belle.'

'I would never have let you come alone,' I said, my eyes

flicking to the house, its dark windows staring out at us like hollow eyes.

A mischief danced in her expression. 'I would have come anyway!'

And I knew it too. Lizzie had no fear. Or rather, she felt fear, but acted in spite of it. That was true courage.

Her eyes raked over the house. 'Was that Mercury? At the door?'

'I think so. He's gone back inside!'

A wide smile lit up her face: her hands flew up to her cheeks. 'I knew it! I knew he was here! We need to find a way in and get him out!'

'We'll need another horse,' I said, looking back towards the wood where Venus was tethered.

Lizzie nodded decisively. 'Mercury can take one of theirs. Did you see the man in the coach with Dupont and Gainsborough?'

I shrugged. It had been hard to get a decent look at him. 'Briefly. Tallish, slender build, masked . . .'

A light was cast on the path where we stood. Someone was slowly lighting lamps in a room on the ground floor. Was it Mercury? I pulled Lizzie into the shadows at the side of the house where we wouldn't be seen.

'We need to get inside,' she said, moving away from me into the darkness. 'Let's try that way.'

We crept around the side of the house into a garden at the back.

The garden was edged with overgrown bushes, their twisted thorny branches clinging to one another in spiky embraces, forming a forbidding wall. Flowers loomed all around us, lush in pink, purple, magenta, violet, indigo, their cupped heads lolling heavily on thick stems. Some had rigid waxy petals; others held clusters of bells, or sprouted spikes like tiny vicious tongues.

I thought of the gardens at Kenwood: ordered, ornate but welcoming and pleasant to the senses. This garden seemed to hold a thousand ills in its leaves and flowers.

'We need to find a way inside,' said Lizzie, looking up at the dark windows.

'We need to be careful,' I warned. 'If we get caught it will only make things worse for Mercury.' I scanned the ground floor. In one corner of the back wall was a small, battered wooden door. 'Over there!'

We approached, staying close to one another. Lizzie put her finger to her lips and tried the handle. It opened on to a small kitchen. We stepped in, listened. Heard the far-off sound of men's voices.

The room was warm and thick with the heavy fug of roasting meat, but behind it, something off, as though the meat was past its best. On the wall in front of us were shelves of jars of skinned fruit. Peaches, cherries, oranges and apples; the round balls of skinless flesh glistening in liquid, their sides flattened against the glass. Jars of seeds, labelled 'peach pits', 'cherry stones', 'apple seeds'. Bundles of dried herbs and flowers tied with string hung from metal hooks in the wall.

On another shelf stood a row of tall glass vials, filled with dried leaves and cut flowerheads and meticulously labelled in small, neat handwriting:

Atropa belladonna / Deadly nightshade

Digitalis purpurea / Foxglove

Aconitum napellus / Monkshood

What were all these plants being used for?

The distant sound of voices grew louder: braying, guffawing. The brittle clinking of glasses. We slipped across the kitchen and into a corridor. There was no one in sight, but the corridor was lined with doors on the side of the house that faced the wood. Patches of damp stained the red damasked walls. Cobwebs clung to the corners of the ceiling.

A harsh laugh.

'It's coming from up there,' whispered Lizzie, pointing to a double door.

'Probably the dining room,' I said, thinking of how my own house was arranged.

Outside, a distant rumble of thunder rose and fell, a sound like mountains colliding. The realisation that no one knew we were here gnawed away at me. Whatever might happen, no one was coming after us. We needed to move out of danger, away from the possibility of discovery, and fast.

Behind us lay a staircase, leading upwards.

'This way!' I said, pulling on Lizzie's arm.

The corridor on the upper floor gave on to two doors, positioned above the dining room where the men had gathered. I tried the first one. It opened on to a gallery: a balcony that ran around the edges of the dining room on the floor below. Backs pressed to the walls of bookshelves behind us, we sidled along, trying to stay out of view of the room beneath.

We crouched down and peered through a small gap in the railings at the scene below. We would have to keep silent if we were to remain undiscovered.

At the head of a long mahogany dining table sat a heavy-set man, his thickly fleshed arms stretched out on the table in front of him. His lank grey hair was plastered down to his head with the grease of weeks and his shirt was stained with sweat and food. His cheeks were reddened and he had the fallen eyes of a bloodhound. His mouth was curled into an ugly sneer.

Behind him, a large stag's head gazed glassily out from the wall at the far end of the room, its branched antlers reaching forward in painful twists, its mouth frozen open in a silent death cry. Lined up along the floor beneath the window were four more large stag heads, each sitting in a puddle of silk.

Were they masks? Robes?

In the centre of the table stood a huge silver candelabra, holding five candles like long lit fingers. Their light sputtered, spewing tiny puffs of black smoke into the air.

At the other end of the table sat Gainsborough, with Dupont beside him. Gainsborough's forehead glimmered with sweat. He tapped lightly on the table with one finger, not taking his eyes off his host.

The rest of the table was obscured from our view by the balcony we crouched on, but a fourth place setting was just visible. Who else was in that room?

'What did you want to discuss with me?' Gainsborough asked, his voice tight with tension.

The man in the grimy shirt held his glass of wine up to the light, narrowed his eyes, then tipped back his head, emptying the glass in one go. He set it down on the table and clicked his fingers.

Mercury appeared from the corner of the room and refilled the glass with a trembling hand. He wore a purple turban topped extravagantly with a large black feather, but his face was ashen, his frame not just lean but bony.

Lizzie gave out a small gasp at the sight of him, whispered his name under her breath. Her face was etched with concern, shot through with relief. I pressed a finger to my lips, shook my head. If we were caught now, Mercury would have no chance of escape.

Mercury stepped cautiously around the table, slowly refilling the glasses with wine, his eyes lowered. He moved with the steady deliberation of one trying not to draw attention to themself, his gestures small, his face an impenetrable mask.

Then he bowed his head and stepped back into the shadows.

Chapter Twenty-Three

The man in the stained shirt stood up and walked to the window, his footsteps marking a slow steady beat on the dark floorboards.

'What does the artist fear?' he opined, staring through the glass at the driving rain. 'Poverty! Hunger! The thought of not being able to feed his hungry children.' He turned to face the artist. 'We, Gainsborough, can keep the wolf of hunger from your door. You are currently England's most favoured portrait painter,' he continued, with mock grandiosity. 'Your star is on the rise!'

Gainsborough shifted in his seat. I pressed myself a little further back towards the wall behind us, tapped Lizzie's arm for her to do the same.

'Everyone wants to see Gainsborough's work and everyone wants to be seen in his work.' The man speaking puffed up visibly. 'To feature in a Gainsborough portrait is to have power, wealth and prestige!'

'That's not my reason for doing the work,' returned the artist. 'I wish to capture personality in paint. To create –'

'Yes, yes, we know!' barked the older man dismissively, waving his glass about, sloshing crimson wine on to the wooden floor. 'But we can make you far wealthier than you had imagined!' He began to pace the room. 'I commissioned you to paint a portrait of me and my son – Rupert.'

Gainsborough glanced towards the man seated to his left, hidden in shadow. I could just make out a grey-gloved hand drumming its fingers gently on the table. The man who had brought them in the coach.

'Father and son with, of course, the necessary inclusion of the boy – our living property.'

People, not property, said the voice in my head.

The speaker waved his arm at the shadows where Mercury lingered. 'The portrait will go on display at the Grand Exhibition and will be entered for the Portrait Prize at the Royal Academy. You will win hands down, there is no doubt.'

He stopped in front of one of the stag heads on the wall, raised a hand to sweep a cobweb from its antlers. He rubbed his thumb and forefinger together. 'We have removed any serious competition. The young upstart woman from Kingston – her work has been . . . dealt with. On winning, you will become the most influential and important portrait artist of the age!'

Lizzie threw me a glance just as his meaning dawned on me. So Miss Harry *had* been sabotaged!

'And what is that to you, a Member of Parliament?' Mr Gainsborough seemed to struggle to keep his voice steady.

The man spun on his heel to face Gainsborough. 'It is not just for me that you will paint, but for the Brotherhood of Masters. A band of brothers. In business, politics, culture . . .'

He waved his hand vaguely towards the library of books behind us. I froze.

'Our system depends on the exchange of favours,' he said expansively.

I exhaled silently and slid my eyes towards Lizzie, who was staring straight ahead of her, wide-eyed.

'You do something for us, we do something for you.' He spread his arms wide. 'Take a lawyer in the Brotherhood, for example. We can send cases his way – he makes more money. And if any of us ever find ourselves in legal difficulties, well, he can help us out! You may have a friend who's a doctor? We can send him patients.'

He smiled then – a sneering, twisted look. 'And if we ever need medical assistance, or perhaps some kind of medical . . . *intervention*, let's say . . . then he can help. And cover our tracks.'

Intervention? The word made me uneasy. What kind of *intervention?*

'So what do you want with me?' Gainsborough's voice was dogged, impatient.

'You will paint power portraits of any member of the Brotherhood that wishes it. And we will reward you in return. Your portrait of myself and Rupert, when it is complete, will give us more prestige and power. Generations to come will see that portrait and know that we wielded power over others.'

The man sat back in his chair, hands clasped across his stomach. 'In turn I can introduce you to wealthy patrons who will employ you to make more art – the wealthiest, perhaps! Even the king himself. Who knows? With more commissions, you make more money. And so on.'

'It's corruption,' said Gainsborough, narrowing his eyes.

'It's advancement,' returned his host. 'See it as a form of promotion. A handshake, a favour, an agreement between gentlemen.' He gave out a harsh laugh, an ugly sound. 'Let's say that my brothers and I have certain . . . financial interests. My businesses all rely heavily on the slave trade. Without slavery, my fortunes cannot survive.'

He placed his hands palms down on the table, leaned forward.

'I want people to remember my name,' he snarled. 'I want them to remember that I was once a master of many!' He brought his fist down on the table. Mercury jumped. 'But your resistance to paint the boy into the picture, on his knees as I have requested, angers me. Other artists have done this, using him in portraits for others. Why should you be any different?'

The man leaped out of his chair now, staggering towards Gainsborough. 'Do you know how many slaves have run away since Mansfield's Somerset ruling?' he growled. 'How much money we have lost in property?'

A muscle flickered in Gainsborough's jaw.

'The Brotherhood believe in Africans as property!' his host spat, flecks flying from his mouth. 'And we will fight to the death to protect our rights over our property.'

I bit my lip in order to keep silence. I felt sick to my stomach.

'Why do you think we rid the world of the Mansfield-Sancho Portrait? What a travesty! Equality? Unity? Ha! Giving them ideas above their station, I call it! And as for Mansfield himself . . . he's a disgrace. The law should be on our side, working with us! Not protecting the runaways! Isn't that so, Rupert?'

'Quite so.' This from the grey-gloved man, softly spoken, but not without menace. His voice was familiar, somehow, but I dismissed the thought from my mind. I did not know anyone called Rupert.

'So you will paint the boy as I have requested,' Rupert's father asserted with finality.

'And if I refuse?' Gainsborough ventured, wiping his face with a handkerchief and returning it to his coat pocket. 'It's not . . . it's not what I wish to be known for.'

The host grasped Mercury hard by the arm. Mercury flinched, resisted, but the man was too strong for him. Lizzie made as if to move forward – I tugged on her shirt to pull her back. Horrible as this was to witness, our invisibility was Mercury's only hope of escape.

'I own this boy!' he roared, holding Mercury in an iron grip, shaking him like a rabid dog with a young hare clenched between its jaws. Mercury struggled to break free. 'He belongs to me!'

Lizzie's breath came thick and fast beside me, her hands balling silently into fists at her sides. I laid a hand gently on her shoulder to calm her.

'I paid good money for him!' the man ranted. 'My family have owned his family for generations! They've tried to break free from us. They always try to break free.' His lips pulled back into a self-satisfied grimace. 'But we always find a way to bring them back. He's mine, and I want him painted that way! I will go down in history as a master! After that, the devil with him. I'll sell him to work sugar in Barbados!'

He pushed Mercury roughly away from him. Mercury fell violently, landed face down on the ground, spreadeagled. The turban slipped from his head and rolled across the floor.

There was no sound but that of the man's panting as he stood, hands fisted, over the fallen boy. My eyes grew hot. Lizzie's face was wet with silent tears.

Mercury dragged himself along the floor, and using the wall for support, stood, slowly, on shaky legs. He lifted his head high but his face betrayed no emotion as he retreated into the corner of the room, rubbing his arm.

'And if you continue to refuse,' Mercury's aggressor wheezed, sinking into his chair once more, 'it shall go hard with you, Mr Gainsborough.'

Gainsborough turned warily to the silent, grey-gloved son, still hidden from our view. Both remained silent.

The older man spoke again, now, his voice slow and slurred. 'We shall speak no more of this. You will finish the portrait tomorrow, the boy included, or your family will have a visit from my son. He will not send a calling card ahead of his arrival. But you will know for certain when he has been.'

Chapter Twenty-Four

A terrible silence followed.

A bitter taste leaped into my mouth. Lizzie wiped the tears from her face with the back of her hand. Gainsborough stared into the fire, his knuckles to his mouth, his face drained of colour. The flames jumped and flickered, casting ribbons of orange light around the room; the wood crackled and spat in the grate.

My mind was reeling from what we had just witnessed.

So the Brotherhood of Masters were slave owners. And they were Mercury's captors, keeping him here to make power portraits for their fellow slave traders or anyone they wished to offer a favour.

Furthermore, they had stolen our portrait so that no one would see us as we would wish to be seen: as equals. It posed a threat to the very institution of slavery! And the idea of a successful woman artist – proud of her African blood – had riled them to violence. They had ransacked her studio and destroyed her work.

The man who had just attacked Mercury and threatened Mr Gainsborough's family picked up the wine bottle from the table and shook it. 'More wine,' he grunted.

Mercury took the empty bottle and turned to leave the room.

Here was our chance! Lizzie and I both moved instinctively, slipping out of the room and flying down the stairs as Mercury disappeared through a door at the end of the corridor.

My chest was packed tight with terror. To follow him we would have to pass the dining-room door. But Lizzie was already halfway up the corridor now, and I had no option but to follow her along that dimly lit passageway, through the door at its end to a narrow stone staircase that spiralled downwards.

The sound of Mercury's footsteps grew more distant as he disappeared into the gloom. Down we went after him, down into the darkness, until we found ourselves in a cellar. Stone walls loomed on either side of us, a low ceiling above our heads. There was no sound but the faint dripping of water from the walls.

'Hello?' Lizzie's voice, tentative, tremulous, floated off into the gloom.

Silence.

Cobwebs dangled from the ceiling and draped themselves over our hair and our shoulders as we proceeded through the darkness. There was no light but for the faint candlelight from the corridor at the top of the stairs behind us.

'Mercury!' hissed Lizzie.

'Who's that?' The voice sounded incredulous. 'Lizzie . . .?'

A match was struck. A flame bloomed on top of a candle and Mercury came into sight, eyes alight with hope. He took a step towards Lizzie, who moved as if in a dream towards him.

His hair had been shorn close to his head, so roughly that there were patches where the skin showed through. Lizzie tentatively lifted a hand to his cheek, as though to make sure he were real.

'Mercury . . .' she whispered.

The boy's face shone. 'Lizzie! Can it really be . . .?'

Choking back a sob, he drew her towards him in the tightest of hugs. Lizzie threw her arms up around him and they stood for a silent moment, wrapped in friendship woven even more tightly now after so many weeks of separation.

I looked at the ground, wishing to give the moment the privacy it deserved.

'I thought we might never see each other again, Lizzie,' Mercury whispered, pulling back and wiping his face.

'How did you find me? I don't even know where we are!'

Lizzie turned to me. 'Belle rode here and I jumped on to the carriage with the artists – oh, sorry! Belle, Mercury; Mercury, Belle.'

Mercury nodded at me, smiled disarmingly. 'Any friend of Lizzie's is a friend of mine.'

Guilt and gratitude battled inside me. 'We have a horse,' I said, conscious that we all needed to get out of there. 'If you can get another we can leave straight away. But we must be quick!'

Mercury paused to think. 'Let me refresh the glasses and plates upstairs. Then I'll tell them that I need to tend to the horses. They always grow skittish in thunderstorms. Wait here a moment!'

He disappeared through a door at the other end of the cellar.

'Mercury!' Lizzie called after him.

'We need to get going, Lizzie,' I warned. I had left Venus for so long in the woods now, I had no idea what kind of state we would find her in. How confident a rider was Mercury? Could he take Lizzie with him if Venus was too troubled?

Mercury appeared again, breathless, holding a cloth bag. 'Here! Take this for me!' Inside was a shirt and a stack of papers, bundled together in the form of a book. 'It's a diary,' he explained.

'Brilliant!' said Lizzie, taking it from him. 'This could be used as evidence against them!'

'Our horse is tethered to an ash tree in the woods,' I told Mercury urgently. 'Just the other side of the stream.'

'I know it,' he said with a nod. 'I'll be there as soon as I can!'

Lizzie grabbed him again in a quick hug. 'Be careful, Mercury. Don't let them see you.'

Mercury raced back up the stairs then, full of an energy fired no doubt by the knowledge that he would soon be free.

'Come on!' I said to Lizzie. 'We'll see him outside.'

She looked doubtful. 'Maybe we should wait near the house. What if he has trouble leaving?'

Footsteps overhead. Time was running out.

'You heard what he said! He'll sort it.' I pulled Lizzie with me up the steps. 'Come on, Lizzie – if you and I get caught, none of us are going anywhere!'

Outside, the relentless rain hammered down in sheets, making treacherous mud of the ground. We slipped and slid as we ran to the woods. There, sheltered in part by the trees, we crouched down and watched the house. The lights were still on in the dining room.

A tall shadow passed across the window. The front door opened, throwing a shaft of dim yellow light across the entrance. A shadow filled the doorway.

'There he is!' said Lizzie. 'He's coming!'

She stood up and waved her arms as the figure came out of the house. But it was taller than Mercury. And as it stalked towards us, I saw that this person, this man too tall to be Mercury, was carrying a large shotgun.

Lizzie staggered backwards, stumbled. The man raised the gun to his shoulder with grey-gloved hands and a loud shot rent the air. A flock of birds shook out of a nearby tree and wheeled off into the night sky.

I grabbed Lizzie's hand and we ran towards the tree where I had tethered Venus. The horse bucked and stamped, her eyes wide with terror. I grabbed on to her reins with one hand, tried to calm her with other. Her hide was freezing to the touch.

'Where's Mercury!' cried Lizzie, looking around frantically. 'Why is he not here?'

There was no sign of Mercury anywhere. Something had gone terribly wrong! Had he been caught?

'We've got to keep moving, Lizzie!'

I swung up on to Venus's back. Lizzie hesitated, still scanning the front of the house for her friend.

'Come on!'

Reluctantly, she clambered up behind me.

'Put your arms around my waist and hold on tightly!' I ordered. 'As though your life depended on it!' I did not need to say out loud what we both knew: that her life, mine and Mercury's, really did depend upon it.

I steered Venus around and turned to look over my shoulder. Still the tall man walked steadily towards us. I kicked Venus into action and we began to gallop away from the house.

Another shot rang out; the bullet whizzed past my head. Venus reared up with a whinny, her eyes rolling with fear. I grasped her neck and clamped my legs about her middle as tightly as I could.

'Don't let go of me, Lizzie!' I started to say, but already

her arms were sliding from me and she hit the ground with a thump.

Lizzie!

My breath stopped.

Panic flooded through me. Venus's front hooves hit the ground again, jerking me forward in the saddle.

Where was she?

Another shot cracked open the sky above our heads, louder this time, closer. Venus skittered sideways and I pulled hard on the reins to wheel her around in a circle while I scanned the ground for Lizzie.

There she was, lying motionless in a crumpled heap a few yards away.

And now, walking towards us with a firm determined stride, our merciless hunter, moving closer and closer, silhouetted against the moonlight. I slipped my hood over my head. Lizzie sat up wide-eyed. I wheeled Venus around once more and Lizzie stumbled to her feet. Venus was cantering away from her now, and she had to run alongside to catch up.

As I reached down, she grasped my hand and I pulled with all the strength I could muster. She seemed to fly on to Venus's back behind me and I snapped the reins hard so that Venus broke into a gallop, hooves striking the ground like a rolling landslide.

I turned to see the figure level the gun against his shoulder once more; then snapped my head back to keep Venus flying forward and away from there, away from the dark woods, from the stinking garden, from the stone house, from Gainsborough and Dupont, from the Brotherhood of Masters – and, as was now painfully clear to us, from Mercury.

Chapter Twenty-Five

Exhausted and spent, silent with shock and disbelief that we had left Mercury behind, it took us several hours to find our way home again.

Lizzie clung to me as Venus limped along. Every fibre in my body twinged and ached. I concentrated all my energy on getting us home, but I had no idea where we had been, and we seemed to circle for hours before we found a crossroads indicating that we were three miles from London.

From there we plodded on until we crested a hill that revealed the city skyline down below. Finally I had my bearings. From here, my house lay to the west.

We rode slowly on to Kenwood, turning off Hampstead Lane up the path to the stables, the soft black night sky above us dotted with pinpricks of silver stars.

I dismounted, then lifted Lizzie down from Venus's back.

As she landed, she yelped with pain. She must have twisted her ankle when she fell. Passing her arm over my shoulders, I supported her into the house and up the back stairs. As we passed the little room I had prepared for Mercury, I felt a twist of loss.

We continued slowly and silently along the corridor to my bedroom, taking care not to wake Aunt and Uncle. Lizzie could spend the night here and return to Sancho's when it was safe to do so in the morning. I helped her into the room and she lay down on the bed, turning on to her side. Her face was streaked with tears; her eyes stared into the distance as I pulled up the coverlet over her. She did not utter a word.

I tucked Mercury's bag under my pillow, lay down beside Lizzie on my back and stared at the ceiling, held in a state of shock, until I drifted off.

Sleep that night was fitful and full of fears. A man with the head of a stag stalked my dreams. The look of despair on Lizzie's face as Mercury turned away from her and ran back into a dark cellar in a house with windows like hollow eyes.

It was obvious to me now that we had taken on a foe far more dangerous than we had ever imagined. This was not simply the case of a stolen painting: a clumsy smash and grab attempt to steal a valuable object. Nor was it a single act of sabotage by an individual, a rival hoping to win a competition. This was something broader, deeper, more complex.

The Brotherhood of Masters wielded power that reached far beyond our own. They were cruel: this much we had heard. They were wealthy: this much we had seen. The Brotherhood of Masters had members everywhere. And they would do anything to protect the trade that gave them power over people like us.

Mercury's Diary

I was sold at the Jamaica Coffee House for ten guineas to a man who said that he had good work for me. His eyes were bloodshot and he smelled of rum and stale sweat. Said that I was one of the lucky ones because I would remain in England. No sugar plantation for me. Easy work. Out in the country. Fresh country air, keep you healthy, he said. Then he slapped me on the back as though we were friends. Or as though I were his horse.

He blindfolded me, bundled me into a coach and we travelled that night to this place. Along many roads, into woods, to this house.

A house, but no home. Only the mice and those men for company. They barely feed me.

Sometimes another one comes here. A younger one. His son? I hear them arguing. They fight like rats over rubbish.

I have taken pencil and paper from them. I will write it all down. They think I cannot read or write. I heard them saying so. They talk about me but they don't know anything at all about me, or care to. I wouldn't tell them anyway.

Boy, fetch this . . . Boy, bring that!

I clean the house, I cook the food, I wait on them hand and foot.

But they forget I have eyes and ears. I am watching. I am listening. And I know them for what they are. I know them all right by what they do.

They keep me in a room in the basement. I sleep on a wooden board with a ragged blanket. At night I dream of emerald green forests where birds of turquoise and scarlet flash through the trees.

I had a mother once, long ago. A father too.

Distant memories: his eyes, twinkling as he woke me in the morning. Her voice, singing, singing to me at night.

These men say I am theirs. That I belong to them. But it's not a belonging like family. It's like an iron chain. The older one, the one that bought me, has a nasty streak. He is quick to temper. The son is the plotter and the planner. He comes and goes. He tells his father to be patient.

They are definitely up to something. They talk about money. They talk about the law.

They don't like each other much.

I eat when they are not looking, but I have to be careful. They keep count of everything.

I only get to change my clothes when it is time for another painting. Yes, then it's all show. People come to the house and choose their props. Some like to hold a gun. Others lie on the grass with a book open. Some stand next to their horse. And then there's me. They give me oil to polish my skin with, a shirt of white silk, a purple turban with an ostrich feather, gold earrings to wear. A costume. It's not real. No one really dresses like that. It's all for show.

They make me kneel or crouch beside, looking up, always up at someone who does not look at me. They give me a tray of fruit to hold. I hold it up, hold it for hours towards people who do not look at me. The fruit smells good but I am not allowed to eat it. Plums, cherries, peaches. My stomach rumbles.

After each painting they gorge. Madeira wine, Jamaica rum, chicken, goose, turtle, candies, chocolates. They send me back to the cellar and they eat and drink and eat and drink for hours and hours and then they sleep.

One day I am going to get out of here. I will find Lizzie again. And I will tell everyone about what happens here. And then I am going to do the things I want to do. Grow the plants I would like to grow. I think I have a knack for it. For cooking too. I know that there is more to life than this.

I am not just a boy in a painting.

I am so much more than a boy in a painting.

NOTES on
The Case of the Purloined Portrait

- Crime: The theft of the Mansfield-Sancho Portrait
- Victims: Miss Harry (as artist), Mansfield family (as owners), both families (as sitting subjects)
- Scene of the crime: The Great Library at Kenwood House
- Time and date: July 1777 at the Masquerade Ball

Notes on the incident:

- A hooded, masked figure broke into the library – from the gardens? – at Kenwood House
- They took the portrait and left via the south-facing window on to the slopes at the back of the house
- Spotted by witness Mr James Knight, they took off down the slopes and escaped across the Heath, possibly to an accomplice waiting with transport

Information sources so far:

- Inspector Meecham
- Mr James Knight, student of law

Possible motives:

- Money? How much might the portrait be worth? Does the thief intend to sell it?
- Professional jealousy? Is the thief a rival artist of Miss Jane Harry's?

Next steps:

- Interview Miss Harry. What else does she know?
- Establish possible rivals

The portrait was stolen by the men at the house in the woods
But how? And who are they?
Where is it? They spoke of getting 'rid' of it

CRIME: Mercury's abduction
Mercury 'bought' at auction by the older man seen at dinner with Gainsborough

Who is he?
- Member of Parliament
- Gainsborough commissioned to create a portrait to show this man as a 'master'

Who is the son?
- Travelled in the coach with Gainsborough and Dupont
- Grey gloves
- Shot at us in the woods

Stag's head crest – which family does this represent? Stag / deer / antlers significance??
- Research ongoing

Where is the house?
- To the north of London
- Estate and gardens

Dear Lizzie,

You must be devastated after yesterday's events.

We have to find out who these men are as quickly as possible and find our way back to that house, back to Mercury – but this time with backup. We can't go in alone again. It's just too dangerous.

I've been thinking over all the clues we found there that might help us.

First of all – who are these men? What is their family name? Sometimes large houses like that are named after the family.

I've found a book of family crests and signets. Each large, land-owning family in the country has a crest or a symbol that represents them. Sometimes the crest is a picture of what the family does for a living or what they grow on their land. I've been trying to match the emblem of the stag's head with a crest, but no joy so far. I'll keep going, though. Perseverance is key!

Here at home, Uncle is feeling rather sick and has had to take to his bed. Aunt Betty has insisted that he take a proper rest from his work.

Have you noticed the numbers of runaway advertisements in the papers at the moment? It is as The Stag said – for so I have taken to calling that horrible man. We are seeking our freedom in ever greater numbers and running away from the people who believe themselves to be our masters and mistresses.

Apparently, Mr Knight will continue to work here while Uncle is ill. He says he does not want Uncle to worry and worsen. He will take on Uncle's runaway cases: helping to make sure that when people run away from their enslavers, they cannot be recaptured to be sent out of the country – rather like the case of Mr James Somerset.

I am hoping this is good news for the Sons and Daughters of Africa.

Please send my good wishes to your family.

Yours always,

Belle

Dear Belle,

I cannot stop thinking about Mercury. He haunts all my dreams.

We must act! Let's go to the Gainsboroughs. They know who was in that room. And maybe they can tell us where the house is. Something, anything.

If you can, meet me at the shop tomorrow and we shall go together.

Best,
Lizzie

P.S. I am really sorry to hear about your uncle. Please wish him well from all of us here. Papa and Mama have asked if there is anything we can do? Should they visit?

When I arrived at the shop, Mrs Sancho waved me over from behind the counter where she was weighing tea leaves and talking in hushed tones with a woman I'd not seen before. A woollen cloak drawn tightly around her and a hood over her head, she sat up at the counter with her hands wrapped around a steaming mug.

'Belle!' Mrs Sancho scooped some dried green leaves into a jar and set the jar on the shelf behind her. 'You here for Lizzie? She'll be down presently. Take a seat, angel.'

I obliged, glancing around the room to see who else was in. Since the SDOA meeting I had felt slightly nervous about being here. Knowing that some people believed I was not to be trusted was not a comfortable feeling. There were several customers seated at tables around the room, but no one paid me much attention.

'May I offer you some chamomile tea?' asked Mrs Sancho, lifting a cast-iron kettle that steamed from its spout. 'Chamomile flowers settle the nerves, calm the mind. I made one for Lizzie this morning – she seem so distress!'

The woman at the counter nodded and hummed in agreement.

The jars on the wall behind Mrs Sancho were packed with dried flowers, tea leaves, herbs and roots. Chamomile, peppermint, ginger, turmeric. A memory flickered in my mind. The kitchen in the house in the woods. The jars with the strange names.

'Thank you, Mrs Sancho,' I said as I took the warm cup from her slender-fingered hands. 'Mmmm, it's good.'

'Chamomile got soothing properties, you know,' said the hooded woman. 'It's a member of the daisy family.' She turned to look at me. There was something about the shape of her eyes that was familiar.

'I'm Belle,' I said, offering a hand.

'Morning, Belle,' she said, taking another sip of her tea.

A silence followed. I tried again. 'Do you know all the properties of these teas?'

'The earth shares her secrets willingly with those who desire to know,' she said. 'The power to heal any wound is always within reach, if we know where to look and if our heart is open to healing.'

'Lord knows we all need some deep healing right now,' Mrs Sancho said wearily, casting her eye over the day's newspaper. 'We got more people breaking free and running from their captors. But captors snatching people back and shipping them like Somerset never happened! And the lies they telling about us in the newspapers! It's like they don't want slavery to end!'

She folded the paper, set it down and turned to me.

'How's your uncle doing, Belle? Lizzie tell me he's sick. You want to take him some chamomile from us?' She spooned some of the flowers into a paper bag and handed it to me. 'There. That might settle him down a little.'

'Thank you, Mrs Sancho . . .'

I slipped the tea into the pouch on my shoulder. No matter what was going on around us, Mrs Sancho always reminded me that we were stronger together. That when you had friendship in the mix, any problem could be shared, any trouble could be faced. So long as Lizzie and I kept working together, we could find Mercury and bring him home, I was certain of it.

'So you met Mama's new friend,' said Lizzie as we crossed the park towards Schomberg House. The storm of two nights ago had cleared the air and a fresh cool breeze blew through the trees above our heads.

I nodded. 'Yes, but who is she?'

'Mama won't say. Apparently her identity has to be kept secret for now. Which suggests she's a runaway. Or a freedom seeker, I should say. That's what Mama says they really are.'

'Maybe Mercury will run . . .' I said, but regretted it instantly.

Lizzie and I had not yet broached the subject of what may have happened to Mercury after we had failed to rescue him. Had he been caught trying to escape? If so, he almost certainly would have been punished. The thought of it was too painful.

We walked in silence for a few moments, taking in the enormity of Mercury's predicament. If that horrible man carried out his threat, then once the portrait was complete, Mercury would be shipped out to a sugar plantation to work for the rest of his life. Did Gainsborough fully realise the fate Mercury faced if he finished that painting?

As we approached Schomberg House I shuddered at the memory of our last trip there.

Lizzie and I had agreed to begin the conversation with an innocent enquiry about Miss Harry's missing portrait. It seemed perfectly reasonable to ask the Gainsboroughs if they had any information as to where the painting might be, or who might have stolen it. At this stage they might at least be willing to hint at where we could find it. From there we could move on to questioning about Mercury and the men holding him.

It was with that thought in mind that I knocked on the door, boldly. There was no response.

Lizzie banged this time, louder, more insistent.

'If it's the Gainsboroughs you're looking for, loves, they've gone!'

I stepped back and looked up. A blond-haired, freckle-faced young woman in a white cloth cap was leaning over the second-floor balcony, attacking a brightly patterned Turkish rug with a wooden carpet-beater.

'Gone? Gone where?' shouted up Lizzie, shielding her eyes from the sun with her arm.

'Didn't say,' the girl chirruped. 'Just packed up, quick as you like, said they were taking a break out in the country.'

'Did they say when they'd return?'

'They didn't, but they took most everything but the kitchen sink with them. I'm not expecting them back any time soon! All right for some, isn't it!'

'Argh!' Lizzie kicked at a pile of rubbish and stormed off up the street.

'Lizzie! Stop!' I tugged at her arm. 'Where are you going?'

She shook me off in a flash of irritation. 'I don't know! What are we going to do? How are we going to find the house? How are we going to get back to Mercury if you can't remember the way?'

My hands went to my hips. 'Lizzie! I was concentrating on following the carriage, remember. And staying out of sight! And thanks to your last-minute stunt, on top of all that I had to watch you into the bargain, in case you fell off the back! So no, Lizzie, I'm sorry, but I really don't know how to get back there!'

She began to walk away, her hands clasped behind her head. She was so restless! Then she stopped, sighed visibly, and turned back towards me, hands thrust into her pockets. She toed a small stone into the road, keeping her eyes firmly fixed on it as she spoke quietly. 'When Mercury first went missing, I didn't even realise!' Her voice was wracked with guilt. 'I . . . I thought he was skipping work or . . . I don't know what I thought. But I didn't look for him.'

She glanced up the road. Carriages rolled past and people strolled arm in arm under twisting pastel-coloured parasols as though they had not a care in the world.

'It didn't occur to me for a moment that he was actually

missing, Belle! And then we saw that poster, remember? At the meeting of the Sons and Daughters of Africa. He'd been taken. My friend. Taken!'

She slid down the wall to her haunches and hid her face in her hands.

'He'd managed to survive here, even without his family, Belle! But then when he needed help, the one person he could rely on let him down!'

She rested her chin on her arms.

'He came here from Jamaica,' she said, her voice distant. 'His parents were involved in a rebellion on a plantation. They took to the hills with hundreds of others. But the British sent soldiers to flush them out. His father was killed. His mother gave him to an African sailor and asked him to take Mercury to London.'

She sniffed. 'He was only seven when he arrived. Seven! He's managed to survive all that time, without a mother, without a father. People love him because he's sweet and he's funny. So he's always got by. And then he got himself a job, earning money, a place to stay. Until . . .'

'He was snatched and put up for auction,' I whispered. I crouched down beside her and took one of her hands in mine.

'And now I've lost him – again!' Lizzie shook her head. 'He was right there, Belle! I actually had him in my arms for a moment. And he's gone again. And it's all my fault. And until he's safe, don't you dare even try and tell me it isn't!'

I knew about guilt. The truth of it was, I felt so guilty for not knowing the way back to the house, it had been keeping me awake at night.

'We should go to Meg,' I said finally, getting to my feet.

She squinted up at me, shielding her eyes from the sun. 'Oh no!' she said in dismay. 'No way! Do you realise how angry she's going to be when she finds out what we've done?'

She was right of course. Meg had said 'on no account' attempt to go on a search and rescue without backup from other members of the SDOA. But what choice did we have?

'We just have to face that, Lizzie,' I said, matter-of-factly. 'But she'll know what to do next. She'll be able to take a more . . . strategic approach.'

Lizzie stared straight ahead for a moment, wrestling with her own thoughts. Then she exhaled deeply, grabbed my hand, and allowed me to pull her up to her feet.

'All right then, if you say so,' she sighed. 'I guess at this time, she'll probably be over at the Dog and Duck.'

Chapter Twenty-Eight

The Dog and Duck tavern was a Sons and Daughters of Africa safe house on Wood Street, near St Paul's Cathedral. Our first dealings with Captain Meg, the head of the search and rescue team for the Sons and Daughters, had been during our last case. She was at once fierce and fearless, compassionate and kind. The sort of woman you wanted on your side if you were going into battle. It was definitely worth braving her wrath, if it meant being honest with her rather than being found out.

We made our way up the Strand, and on up Fleet Street towards St Paul's Cathedral, the great domed centre of our city, London's glowing heart. The cathedral steps were thronging with people: among them those seeking alms, their hands cupped in the hope of drawing a kindness in coin from a passer-by.

Behind the cathedral, we turned into Wood Street and stopped at the sign of the Dog and Duck.

We found Meg in a low-ceilinged, L-shaped room, playing cards with three men and another woman. As we approached, she spread her hand down on the table with a whoop of triumph. The other card players threw down their hands in disgust. At the sight of us, Meg muttered something in the ear of the broad-shouldered man next to her, who nodded, keeping his eyes on us all the while, and got up.

'Follow me!' she said over her shoulder, as she made her way to the back of the room. Her step was firm, deliberate, her shoulders square. She was every inch a captain. She disappeared through a door into an outside yard, where women were practising hand-to-hand combat. Some, like Lizzie and Meg, wore breeches and shirts. Others wore smocks or work dresses, ripped at the sides to allow for more movement as they lunged and kicked. They worked in pairs, eyeing each other steadily, mirroring and repeating each other's moves.

'Our members need a range of skills,' Meg explained as we passed in between the rows of women and girls, ducking out of the way of the rhythmically jabbing fists and feet.

At the end of the yard, Meg pulled up a barrel, indicating for us to do the same. We sat in a tight triangle, silently watching the women in dance-like combat for a moment.

Then, clearly unable to hold it in any longer, Lizzie launched into the full story of everything that had happened since the theft of the portrait, explaining how we had got a lead from Miss Harry about Gainsborough acting strangely, how we had overheard him and his nephew talking about Mercury and a journey somewhere. How we had followed the Gainsboroughs to the house in the woods, but found Mercury there.

Mercury, and a garden full of rotten, stinking plants and thorny flowers.

Mercury, and the threat of being painted in servitude, then sent to the plantations.

Mercury, and the men keeping him there against his will.

Mercury.

Lizzie wiped a tear from her eye with the back of her hand. Her jaw was set, determined, her expression grim. Meg stared straight ahead, silent. I put my arm around Lizzie's shoulders. I had no words to help her right now.

'So . . .' said Meg after what seemed like an eternity. 'You went into that house alone, without any backup at all, without any protection?' She leaned forward over her knees as she spoke, hands clasped in front of her, eyes narrowed towards the women sawing at the air with alternate hands.

Lizzie sniffed and nodded. 'You said that the Sons and Daughters had to lay low. And . . . and I just wanted to get him out of there.'

'And how did that work out for you, missy?' said Meg, her eyes still fixed on the fighters.

Lizzie glanced nervously at me.

'We thought that with the two of us . . .' My voice came out sounding silly and small.

'I see,' said Meg. 'So *you* were the backup. Didn't have you down as a tough girl, Belle.'

Something inside me shrank a little. I looked over at the women who were practising high kicks to the side, their fists up in front of their faces. It was true that if the confrontation had become physical, I would have been lost.

That being said, I had ridden us out of danger.

'You said that the Sons and Daughters had put a hold on missions!' Lizzie protested. 'You said that they weren't going out for days!'

'With good reason!' Meg retorted, pushing up on to her feet. 'Our people are under attack! We are being ambushed at every turn. Arrested! Have you ever spent time in Newgate Jail? Think you could handle some time in there? Though with all due respect, you, missy –' She shot me a piercing look. 'Well, your uncle would probably have you out of there in a trice, no?'

Knowing she was right, I held my tongue. There was no way that Uncle would suffer me to be thrown in jail. Most people didn't have that kind of protection. Or privilege.

'We just wanted to help!' pleaded Lizzie. 'Didn't you say it was down to all of us to fight?'

'To fight *wisely*!' shot back Meg.

She walked over to a young woman and with deft hands, gently adjusted the set of her shoulders, turned her chin slightly to the side. She tapped the woman's stomach with two fingers. 'Keep your balance in your centre, Clara. Or else she'll have you over with one strike.'

She turned back to us, hands on hips. 'According to your own account, you were chased off that land like rabbits. You could have been killed!' She threw her hands in the air in exasperation. 'How does that help any of us?'

My eyes filled with tears. I fought off the urge to get up and leave.

Meg sighed and crouched down in front of us, grasped each of us by the hand. 'I don't mean to be harsh with you, but . . . this work is dangerous! We do it because we have to. We do it because we don't want to keep losing our people. And that includes you two!'

Lizzie fixed Meg with a look of appeal. 'I am sorry, Meg, really I am,' she said ardently. 'I can't believe we lost Mercury again. And it's all my fault. I'm so worried about him. I can't sleep . . .'

'What you did was brave, girls, and no mistake,' conceded Meg, softening a little. 'Silly brave rather than smart brave, but brave nonetheless. But now we need to get smart and we need to get practical.'

She stood up.

'We need to identify those two men as soon as possible, or locate the house,' she said, tapping her palm with a decisive finger. 'If you were able to give us any more details about the house for me to share with the organisation, it would help. Maybe one of our members has even been held there themselves at some point.'

We both looked at the ground, painfully aware of our woeful lack of strategy.

'Any details at all?' Meg asked, shifting her attention from Lizzie to me.

'The son's called Rupert . . .' I said meekly.

Meg sighed. 'So we'll work with what we have. We're looking for a father and son, slave owners, one of them's a Member of Parliament,' she said. 'Unfortunately it doesn't narrow it down a great deal, but I'll make enquiries. It may be that some of our freedom seekers know these men or the house.'

'Maybe we could come to a meeting and describe the house, the man we saw, to the freedom seekers?' I suggested.

Meg shook her head. 'The freedom seekers live in hiding. Their captors are out there looking for them, so they can't come to meetings. We'd have to find a way to circulate the details. I can start asking around but we could do with more information . . .'

She took something out of her pocket, put it in her mouth and began chewing vigorously as she spoke.

'Meanwhile, it's possible that Mercury may run away and seek his freedom. You girls opened up that possibility for him.' Her tone was thoughtful, philosophical even. 'If he does run, we've got more chance of finding him, I would say. And he has a chance of finding us.'

Meg faced the women in combat training and clapped her hands twice. They stepped back from one another, relaxed, shook hands and placed a fist over their chests.

She turned back to us.

'Our people run away all the time. A fair few of us were enslaved at one point or another. Running away is just one of the ways we resist. Freedom seekers come to us for protection if they can, or we seek them out. Help them to food, lodging, some protection. We can help them to new identities, to blend back into society, to feel safe again, make some kind of life for themselves. It's not often an easy one, but it sure beats the pain and humiliation of living as someone else's property. Plus, if Mercury runs, this so-called Brotherhood will come forward if they want him back.'

'How do you mean?' I asked.

'So-called slave owners hate it when we run away,' said

Meg, with satisfaction. 'To them, it's partly about the money and partly a matter of pride. The way they see it, they've lost a valuable item of property, and they want it back.'

'Plus, who's going to do all their dirty work for them?' Lizzie added.

'Exactly!' returned Meg.

'So what do they do?' I asked. How easy was it to find someone in London if they did not want to be found, I wondered?

Meg's eyes glittered like steel. 'They advertise, honey. They take out an advertisement in the newspaper. Asking for the runaway to be "apprehended" and "returned" to them. Offer a hefty reward too.'

Of course! I had seen many such advertisements for runaways. I had somehow imagined that it was the Bow Street Runners placing them. It had not occurred to me that they were placed by so-called slave owners wanting their property back.

Meg spat a large ball of tobacco into the dirt.

'Without a name or a location for these men, let's hope that Mercury runs,' she said, waving us to our feet. 'That way, if these guys want him back, they're going to have to come out of the shadows and darn well ask for him.'

Chapter Twenty-Nine

'Surely she can't expect us to just wait until Mercury runs away!'

Lizzie was tearing off up Cheapside towards Poultry at a furious pace and I had to jog to keep up with her.

'She said that one of the freedom seekers might know the men or the house . . .' I offered.

'But Belle!' Lizzie stopped in the street and faced me. 'How can we show them either of those things?' She threw up her hands and paced around the middle of the road. 'We can't invite the freedom seekers to a meeting, and we've got nothing to give Meg to show them. No map, no pictures of the men – nothing!'

Then the idea came to me like a burst of brilliant music – a jubilant chord in a Handel oratorio. 'That's it!' I gasped. 'That's what we need! You're fantastic, Lizzie!'

She frowned. 'What?'

I held her by the arms. 'We go to Miss Harry. We describe everything we saw – the house, the woods, the men, everything. She can draw while we describe!'

Lizzie frowned. 'Won't that be super tricky?'

I shrugged. 'Perhaps,' I conceded. 'But she's skilled – and between us I reckon we'll remember enough detail for her to produce something that we can give to Meg. Maybe the Sons and Daughters can even reproduce it for us, like they did for the Mercury posters.'

I could see Lizzie mapping it out in her head. She planted her hands on her hips. 'It could work, couldn't it?'

'It's worth a try,' I said, starting off down the street. 'And right now, it's all we've got!'

As it happened, Miss Harry's lodgings were just a few streets away, in Lombard Street.

Just along from London's Jewish Quarter, Lombard Street was known for its Quaker residents, some of whom had begun to circulate Abolitionist pamphlets. Unsurprising then that Miss Harry had chosen to make her home here. The address she had given us was a modest house, well-to-do but strangely quiet. We were shown into a drawing room where the artist sat in the window-seat, sketching in charcoal on a large piece of paper. So she had not given up working then.

We had agreed that we would tell her everything. We were convinced that the Brotherhood of Masters were behind the theft of her painting, and confident that she would be keen to help us retrieve Mercury from their grasp. Miss Harry listened intently as we took it in turns to recount the story, then nodded. Some unspoken worry seemed to trouble her.

'I am glad you have come to me.' She stood up and walked to the fireplace, playing with the ringlet of hair that snaked over her shoulder. When she spoke, the note of gravity in her voice was unmistakable.

'I feel I must share more with you about why I am here, why it means so much to me to make my own way in the world.' She stared in the looking glass above the fireplace as she spoke. 'You may already know something of my own background.'

What did Miss Harry have to tell us? And why now? Lizzie threw me a worried glance.

'Well,' I began. 'We read that your mother is African and your father English, not unlike my own family . . .'

She smiled, somewhat bitterly. 'That's true. Except my father, Thomas Hibbert, holds people as property.

The Hibberts are one of the wealthiest slave merchant families in Britain.'

Lizzie and I exchanged looks of bewilderment.

Jane Harry lowered her eyes. 'This is the shame I carry,' she said calmly. 'Even my mother, a free woman of African and English descent, runs a plantation in Jamaica. This was to be my inheritance, but I want no part of it. If the plantation is left to me, my plan is to ensure the freedom of those that labour there.'

I could not believe what I was hearing. 'Is this why the Academy were reluctant to accept you?' I asked.

Miss Harry shook her head. 'The irony is that it is not the shameful source of our family's money that bothers those men, but simply the circumstances of my birth. Since my parents are not married, I am a member of what they call an "outside family". And my mother's heritage compounds their contempt for me.'

Of course. It was the Brotherhood who had tried to force Miss Harry out.

Mr Sancho had told us many times that the trade in enslaved people was responsible for a thousand ills. One being that it was 'a great destroyer of families'.

My own mother surfaced in my mind.

Many people talked of my family story as though it were a source of shame. As far as I was concerned, that my parents were unmarried was nothing to be ashamed of. They had loved each other. And that thought brought me comfort. How odd that such a relationship was considered by some more a cause for shame than the practice of enslaving human beings for profit.

Miss Harry wandered the edges of the room, trailing a finger over the spines of the books that lined the walls. 'When I first arrived in England I stayed with family friends: a business partner of my father's and his wife. It was unbearable. The things they said, the things they believed. And they allowed themselves to say those things in front of me because, well, perhaps they imagined I would agree. And so when I befriended the Knowles family, Abolitionists working towards an end to slavery, I asked if I could join them in their home.'

She spread her arms wide. 'And here I am. Among people who believe, as I do, that slavery is a horror that must end! That is precisely why I painted the portrait of you girls with your families. What a story that picture told!'

Her face clouded over with regret.

'So you'll help us then?' asked Lizzie.

'Of course!' said Miss Harry. 'What is the purpose of art if not to be used as a force for change, a force for good? I will. I must.'

'We need you to draw the house and the man we saw exactly as we describe!' I said, suddenly aware again of the urgency of the situation. 'We can share the images with the Sons and Daughters of Africa and maybe identify the family holding Mercury.'

Miss Harry sprang into action. 'Let us not waste another moment!' She set about preparing an easel by the window. 'This isn't going to be pleasant, but I need you to imagine that you're back at the house,' she said, clipping a large sheet of paper to the frame. 'Describe everything you saw. Leave no detail unspoken. I'll do my best to render the images you need.' She took up her charcoals.

Together, Lizzie and I began to describe the journey through the woods, the approach to the house. I shuddered as I saw again in my mind the great manor house towering over us in the moonlight, staring at us with hollow eyes.

Miss Harry's hand moved with such agility, such energy! Her eyes were screwed to the page, narrowed with concentration as we relived the horrible journey through the house, the chilling confrontation between Gainsborough and Mercury's captor. Little by little, the house, the dining room and the Stag all came to life before our very eyes.

'There!' Jane Harry said at last, and turned the easel towards us.

It was uncanny. There was the house, seen from the woods, exactly as though she had been there herself. The back of my neck prickled. As for the Stag, she had captured him perfectly. The thick set of his shoulders and neck, the sneer of his lips, his hound-dog eyes. Seeing his face again brought him back into my mind. The menace, the loathing, the contempt for his fellow human beings. It was a brilliant likeness of a man rotting from the inside out.

'It's strange seeing it all again like that,' Lizzie whispered, moving her hand above the page as though retracing its lines. 'How on earth do you do it?'

Miss Harry blushed. 'Practice?'

'Thank you, Miss Harry,' I said, taking the pages and

rolling them up. 'This could provide the key to it all!'

'I hope so,' said Miss Harry, walking us to the door. 'I've been thinking about Mercury ever since you left his picture with me.' She leaned on the door frame. 'Let's hope the Sons and Daughters of Africa can find the house and get him back soon. And if those men *have* taken the Mansfield-Sancho Portrait, maybe we will see it again after all?'

Back at the Dog and Duck, Meg rolled out the images from Miss Harry.

'Impressive!' she said. 'This woman has skills! We could work with someone like that!'

I slid Lizzie a relieved smile. Having mis-stepped already in Meg's eyes, we were both keen to show that we could help find Mercury again.

'Yeah, this one looks familiar to me,' Meg said, tapping the page. 'He looks like he's full of grudges and bad feeling. I don't know his name. But the house . . .' She shook her head. 'I've not seen it.' She rolled up the images and placed them in a pouch at her side. 'Leave it with me,' she said. 'We'll soon know if any of our freedom seekers know this place. I'll send word to Sancho's as soon as I have news.'

Chapter Thirty

I rode Venus into town so that I could pick up Lizzie on the way to the Dog and Duck. I turned into Charles Street to find her sitting on the kerbside outside Sancho's, elbows resting on her knees. As she stood up to greet me, she eyed

Venus nervously. She clearly hadn't forgotten our frantic flight the other night.

'Don't worry,' I said, smiling and patting Venus's neck gently. 'She'll walk the whole way.' I hauled Lizzie up behind me and we rode along the riverside as far as St Paul's, then turned north towards Wood Street.

Meg greeted us outside the tavern and led us to the stables.

'She's beautiful!' purred Meg, stroking Venus's muzzle as she walked her along. 'She'll be looked after here until we get back.'

We followed her through the stable, then into a long tunnel that went down, down underground, until I believed we must have been at least twenty yards under the streets of the city. The sound of dripping water echoed around us.

At the end of the tunnel we reached a large, arched door, where Meg gave three long knocks, followed by two short ones. Behind the door, a metal bolt slid open. Then another, and another. The door opened a crack, and then wider. A tall man with an angular face and hooded eyes waved us in, nodding to a room behind him.

It was a small cell, lit by a single lantern on the wall. There, on a narrow bed, sat a woman, hands folded in her lap. She looked up as we entered, and in the half darkness I saw that it was the woman I had seen in Mrs Sancho's that day. The one who had talked to me about chamomile.

'This is Aja,' said Meg, stepping back into the corner of the room. 'She'll tell you everything.'

Lizzie stared at Aja as though she recognised her, but couldn't place her.

'Would you mind if I took notes?' I asked, opening up the pouch, and sitting cross-legged on the floor.

'Please,' Aja said, bringing her hands together in front of her, palm to palm. 'I would like my story to be heard.'

Aja's Story

Set down faithfully by Miss Dido Belle, 27th July 1777

My name is Aja. In Jamaica, they called me Sally. I was born in a village on the Guinea coast to an educated Igbo family. Our people are known for our love of music, poetry, dancing. The land there is fresh and fertile, fruitful.

My father was a learned man, a cleric. My mother was a herbalist. She knew all the properties of the fruits and flowers and grasses and herbs that grew in the soil. For her, the earth was a rich kitchen to be loved, worshipped and respected. When she sowed, she planted again. What she took, she replenished. Crucial, she said, for the balance of the land.

I was sold to the man in your picture and send to work on his sugar plantation when I was just ten years old.

There I toiled by day in fields of sugar cane from dawn till dusk, eyes down to avoid the lash. Our master was a cruel man. Prone to violence, and outbursts of furious temper. His closest friend was the whip. It never left his side. The heat seemed to inflame his rage. By night I foraged in the forests, gathering plants and herbs to heal the wounds of my brothers and sisters, mixing medicines to heal them when they were sick.

The master had no respect for the gifts of the earth, but he longed to know its secrets. When he discovered my skills he brought me into the house to work as a cook and a nurse. Years of my life passed in this way.

Then one day my comrades sent whispers rippling through the canefields. A rebellion in planning. When the sign came, we would rise up against our so-called master. Everyone had their part to play. Mine was to concoct a herbal tincture to be slipped into his drink, to make him sleep deeply while we burned the canefields and took to the hills.

Two days later, the message came. It was time. Everything went according to plan. We escaped. Fled to the Blue Mountains and formed our own community.

There, where the clouds wreathed the mountaintops and

the air was fresh and clean to sharpen the mind and bring us back to ourselves, there we made a new life together. We had to keep our wits about us. Stay sharp. They could come for us at any moment. We looked out for one another.

I learned to listen even more carefully to the earth and her secrets. How to spot the readiness of a flower by its lean into the sun, the ripeness of a fruit by the weight of its hang, the gentle give of fruit-skin beneath the press of eager fingers.

I had a family. A man who had toiled alongside me in the canefields, bending and twisting among the tall green stalks. But I had never noticed before the way the sun seemed to dance in his eyes whenever he looked at me.

We had a child together. A beautiful boy. For years we lived on in this way. In the trees overheard, birds flashed turquoise and scarlet and woke us each morning with their music.

When our son was seven years old, a patrol of British soldiers was sent into the mountains to flush us out. A fierce battle ensued. My husband was killed. I escaped only with my life, my child, and the clothes I was wearing.

We ran by night and day until we reached the harbour. I could not get a passage but placed my son into the hands of a sailor, a Yoruba man who promised to take him to England. He knew a community in London who could look out for him. There, I imagined, my child would be free.

It was a terrible risk – the long journey at sea, handing him over to a man I did not know, sending him off into the unknown – but I could not imagine a fate worse than slavery. I believed that if he arrived safe in England, fortune would provide for him. Little did I know the dangers awaiting our people on English shores. I gave my son something to remember me by. Something that would help me to find him when the time came. A bracelet that I had worn since my own childhood, crafted for me by an aunt.

At the harbour I was recaptured and taken to a plantation on the other side of the island. Finally, many years after losing my son, I am here.

In my heart I always believed that he was alive. And I always believed that I would see him again.

Here she paused.

'Mercury,' Lizzie whispered.

'Kofi,' said Aja gravely, leaning forward and thumbing the tears from Lizzie's cheek. 'His name is Kofi.'

Lizzie grasped Aja's hands and stared up at her. When you knew, you could see traces of Kofi in Aja's eyes, in the curve of her lip. Lizzie had believed that Kofi had lost his parents forever. And yet here was his mother in the flesh: alive, and looking for him.

'When the ship I was on docked in Greenwich, I was shocked to see how many people lived here,' Aja said, looking over at Meg. 'That was the first time I feared that I may not find him after all. And then one day I saw a poster. An image of a boy I knew was mine.'

She gave Lizzie a smile warmed by her love for her son.

'I watched you from afar,' she said. 'Going from door to door, pinning up pictures of my child, asking around, asking if anyone had seen him. Everyone kept going about their business, but you persisted. And even before I had found

him, even before I had seen him again, it made my heart
sing to know that my son had found – no, formed – such a
friendship, such a bond of love. A sister, even.'

'We found him!' said Lizzie. 'I had him! But . . .'
She edged closer to Aja. 'We lost him again and I am so sorry.
I am so, so sorry!'

Aja wrapped her arms around Lizzie. 'There, there, girl.
No crying now. You didn't lose him. You led me to him.'

Meg passed Aja the poster of the Stag. 'Tell them, Aja,'
she said.

Aja narrowed her eyes at the image in front of her. Her
mouth became a grim line. 'That's the man I lost so many

years of my life to. Working day in day out with my face turned to the ground. His name is Hartmoor. Hugh Hartmoor.'

She thrust the poster back towards Meg as if wishing to be rid of it.

My mind was whirring. That name. Those initials. I had seen those initials. Hugh Hartmoor. *HH* . . . Of course! That nasty letter in the newspaper! It was signed HH MP – Hartmoor was a Member of Parliament!

'He's the one that has put a price on my head,' said Aja. 'I am still wanted for his poisoning, though all I ever did was put him into a deep sleep.'

'Now that we have his name, it won't take us long to find the house,' said Meg. 'We're gathering together for a rescue mission early tomorrow morning. The timing's tricky, given the current state of affairs, but we need to get Kofi out of there.'

'Where shall we meet?' said Lizzie.

'Oh no!' said Meg. 'You're not coming! We'll report back to you in the morning.'

Lizzie appealed to Aja. 'But we've already been in the house! We know our way around it!'

She turned beseechingly to Meg. Meg pulled on her jacket, shook it on to her shoulders, without taking her eyes off Lizzie.

'I'd say our intelligence was indispensable!' Lizzie added.

I was glad that for once it wasn't me having to go up

against Lizzie when she had an idea.

Meg shook her head as though she couldn't believe what she was about to say. She sighed. 'You girls come, you follow my instructions to the letter.'

I flicked a glance towards Lizzie. This would be easier for me to fulfil than for her.

Meg caught the thought. 'To. The. Letter! Do you hear?'

We nodded, contrite.

'We meet at the Dog and Duck at four, before the sun comes up. I'll brief you then.'

I raced back home on Venus to ready myself for the night's outing. Finally we could return for Mercury – Kofi – with the help that we needed, with some force behind us!

Stronger together.

I ran upstairs to my bedroom, but was stopped by voices coming from Uncle's room. The door was half open, and the sound of someone crying drifted out into the hall.

Uncle was lying in bed, clutching his stomach and groaning. Aunt Betty was sitting on the bed beside him, sobbing into her handkerchief. Mr Knight stood by the window, hands behind his back, a solemn expression etched on to his face.

'Aunt Betty!' I rushed over to the bed. 'What on earth's the matter?' Uncle was pale, his face clammy with sweat. I took hold of his hand to comfort him and flinched at the touch. 'He's freezing!' I gasped.

'Belle, your uncle is very sick.' Aunt Betty's voice was wound tight with anxiety. 'He's in great pain with his stomach: he cannot eat . . .'

'I've called for Dr Simpson,' said Mr Knight with authority. 'He's on his way.'

When Dr Simpson – a short plump man with large, bespectacled grey eyes – arrived, he placed his brown leather bag down on the bedside table and laid his hand on Uncle's forehead. We watched in silence as he listened to his breathing, noted the rise and fall of his chest. He straightened up from the bed.

'Please wait outside, so that I may attend to Lord Mansfield with no distraction. He needs peace and quiet at the very least, as do I in order to carry out my duties.'

He ushered us out of the room. Not wanting to go too far off, I sat on a chair in the hall and kept my eyes on the door. Mr Knight leaned on the wall, brows knitted, lost in his own thoughts. Aunt Betty paced up and down the corridor, her handkerchief grasped to her mouth.

I felt wretched. All this time I had been dashing about town with Lizzie, thinking only of the portrait, of Gainsborough, of Kofi. I had given less and less thought to Uncle since Mr Knight had arrived on the scene. I had assumed he did not need me, had believed that perhaps he wanted me out of the way so that he could continue with his work unimpeded. Aunt Betty had told me he was unwell but I had thought he was simply in need of rest. I had never imagined that it was as serious as this!

At length, Dr Simpson emerged from Uncle's room, energetic in his movements in spite of his advanced years. He took out a cloth from his waistcoat pocket and polished his glasses while he spoke.

'It seems Lord Mansfield is suffering from a violent sickness of the stomach,' he said incisively.

'What do you think is causing it, Doctor?' Aunt was on her feet. 'He seems to be in so much pain!'

Dr Simpson nodded. 'I've given him something for that. But,' he went on, flashing Aunt Betty a cautious look, 'I believe the illness may have been caused by something he ingested.'

'Ingested?'

At the sound of my voice, everyone turned to me, as though remembering for the first time that I was there.

'It means eaten or drunk,' said Dr Simpson, putting his glasses back on.

Aunt Betty hesitated. 'Do you mean poison, Doctor?'

'Surely not!' interjected Mr Knight.

I felt the blood drain from my face. Poison! It couldn't be!

'Well, I don't want to jump to conclusions, but it's a distinct possibility,' said the doctor. 'The suddenness of the attack, the extent of the pain . . .'

Aunt Betty sank back into her chair with a cry of anguish.

'Do you know what the poison is? Or when it was given?' Mr Knight demanded.

Dr Simpson shook his head. 'At this stage, I can't be certain. There are a number of poisons that produce symptoms of nausea and vomiting. It could be any one of these. I'd have to investigate further.' He cleared his throat. 'For clarification, you might have to consult with someone with more . . . criminal expertise.'

'I'll send for Meecham,' said Mr Knight.

I threw Aunt Betty a look of appeal. Why was Mr Knight acting as though he was in charge all of a sudden?

'Meecham? Oh please, not that insufferable man!' cried Aunt Betty. 'There must be someone else who can help!'

Chapter Thirty-Two

Apparently there was not.

According to Constable Meecham himself – or Inspector Meecham now, as he was quick to inform us when he returned with Mr Knight – he was the member of the Bow Street Runners with expertise in poisons.

Dr Simpson and Mr Knight took the Inspector into Uncle's dressing room so that they could share with him the news and details of Uncle's condition. Out of the way of the ladies of course. Heaven forbid we should be exposed to the realities of a situation that affected us so deeply! I hovered by the door, but could only hear the concerned murmur of their voices.

When they emerged, Meecham asked us to stay where we were while he conducted a search of the kitchen to try and identify the source of the poison. I didn't hold out any hope. Meecham didn't seem able to find the nose on his face,

Uncle had once said. How he had managed to get himself promoted was beyond me.

I watched Uncle now, as Aunt Betty and I sat on the bed either side of him, each holding one of his hands. He looked so weak and thin, lying back on the pillow, his chest gently moving up and down. Dr Simpson had given him something to alleviate the pain and help him sleep. Looking at his face in that moment, I would have given anything to see him open his eyes, smile again.

My mind raced in all directions.

When could this have happened? What had he been poisoned with? Who would have wanted to do such a thing?

Voices on the stairs announced the men's return. We stood to greet them as they marched in. Mr Knight's brow was stamped with worry, but Meecham was looking very pleased with himself. Drawing himself up to his full height, he cleared his throat and announced that he had indeed located the source of the poison.

Already?

'You have, Inspector?' Even Aunt Betty could barely mask the surprise in her voice.

Meecham began to strut to and fro at the end of Uncle's bed. 'Judging by the timings of the onset of Lord Mansfield's illness and a close inspection of the kitchens here at Kenwood,' he said pompously, 'we have traced the poison swallowed by Lord Mansfield to a packet of tea that came into the house in a hamper from Sancho's Tea Shop.'

There was a silence while we took in his words. Sancho's Tea Shop?

My blood ran like ice water.

'Well, that can't be . . .' I said with a half-laugh.

Meecham stood firm, hands behind his back, chest out, chin up. Dr Simpson gave a helpless shrug. Mr Knight frowned at the floor, shaking his head.

I turned to Aunt Betty, who was staring, open-mouthed at Meecham.

'It's not possible!' I insisted. 'Aunt! Tell them!'

Stricken, Aunt Betty looked from Inspector Meecham to Mr Knight and to the doctor. Why was she waiting for answers from them? She knew for herself!

I tried again. 'Don't you understand? They're our friends!' Why was I the only person in the room talking?

Aunt Betty was frowning now, clearly as perplexed as I was. 'Are you quite sure, Constable?' she said finally.

'Inspector!' he snapped, indignant.

She fluttered her hand dismissively. 'Yes, yes, Inspector. But I fear there must be some mistake. The Sancho family have become very dear friends to us.'

'But what about those around them, Lady Mansfield?' proposed Mr Knight.

I spun around to face him. He ignored me and continued to address only Aunt Betty.

'I have heard on good authority that Sancho's is overrun with rebels and runaways. And,' he lowered his voice, 'there are those among them who have expertise in poison. It's a common practice in those . . . communities.'

'Whom Uncle is helping through his work!' I protested. And wasn't Mr Knight supposed to be helping them too? 'Why would any of them want to poison him?'

He looked at me, then spoke delicately. 'Perhaps this is not a conversation for . . . I realise there are . . . allegiances . . .'

'I'd like to stay, if it's all the same to you,' I said, straining to keep the courtesy in my tone. 'I know the Sanchos better than anyone here!'

It was absolutely unthinkable that anyone in Lizzie's family would try and hurt Uncle, Aunt or myself. I knew that, and surely so did Aunt Betty.

But another thought gnawed at me.

What about the Sons and Daughters at Sancho's who had believed we might be the source of the leak? Who thought perhaps somehow Uncle – or someone at 'the Mansfield house' – was betraying them to the Bow Street Runners? Was it possible that someone in their midst really did wish Uncle harm?

Meecham of course was the last person on earth I wanted

to be discussing this with, or in front of. And why was he so concerned about upholding the law all of a sudden? He had shown very little interest in finding Mercury or any of the missing members of the Sons and Daughters of Africa and had not felt compelled to do anything about finding our portrait either.

I folded my arms across my chest. 'Which goods exactly are supposed to have been poisoned, Inspector?' There. Let him at least give specifics.

'I believe it is a batch of tea. Sent here in a hamper by Mrs Sancho herself.'

I took a step towards him, faced him squarely. 'What kind of tea?' I persisted.

'Belle, please,' said Aunt, laying her hand on my arm.

'This is clearly distressing for the girl,' said Mr Knight, holding up his hands. 'I suggest we take the conversation elsewhere and allow her to attend to her uncle.'

'We will be searching Sancho's Tea Shop,' Meecham went on, sidestepping me and crossing the room to the door. 'And, if necessary, we will be making arrests.' This last over his shoulder as he left the room, Mr Knight following closely behind.

Aunt Betty rubbed at her temples. 'What have we got ourselves mixed up in?' she murmured to herself as she went after them.

I stood, aghast, trying to collect my thoughts. It was impossible! I pulled a chair up to the side of Uncle's bed and took his hand in mine. If only Uncle were conscious, he would have put a stop to all of this ridiculous talk immediately! He would have known what to say to stop these men pushing ahead with this nonsensical line of enquiry.

But of course he said nothing. He just lay there, motionless, a painful reminder of just how thin the line was between life and death.

DAILY POST

LORD MANSFIELD FEARED POISONED BY REBEL GROUP

The Lord Chief Justice Lord Mansfield has been taken ill at his Kenwood home, feared to be suffering the ill effects of an ingested poison.

The Bow Street Runners visited the house yesterday where they interviewed family members and friends regarding the alarming development.

The wily judge, best known to some for the Somerset ruling of 1772, is reported to be suffering from nausea, excruciating stomach pains and bouts of vomiting. His doctor has confirmed that his condition is now stable.

It is believed that the poison may have originated from a packet of tea sent to Lord Mansfield by the Sancho family, from their Westminster shop. Sancho's Tea Shop is known as a safe haven for political rebels and runaways.

The Bow Street Runners are now conducting a thorough search of the premises and questioning a number of suspects. Spokesman Inspector Meecham said that he expected to make a number of arrests in the next day or so.

Dear Belle,

What on earth is happening?

The Bow Street Runners came to our home this morning and have torn the place apart! They say your uncle is poisoned and that we are the prime suspects!

They ordered everyone into the back room while they searched the premises in a most violent manner, turning over tables and chairs and smashing jars of tea on the floor. Kitty and Billy were absolutely terrified.

Billy won't let Mama out of his sight now for a second.

Mama is in a state of extreme distress. She puts on a brave face in front of us, but I have glimpsed her crying when she thinks no one is watching. Papa is frantically writing letters to his network of friends in an attempt to drum up support from our local community. I have been tasked with delivering these letters. You learn very quickly who your real friends are when trouble is at your door.

And Kofi's rescue mission has been called off! Meg said that the house where he is being held is called Hartmoor Hall. But now, nearly all the members of the Sons and Daughters of Africa have been pulled in for questioning by the Bow Street Runners; those in hiding have had to go to ground.

Belle, how could they suspect us of such a thing?

You have to tell them that the poison did not come from here!

I wanted to come and see you but Papa says I am not to until this is all cleared up. He says it may make matters worse for us. I overheard him arguing with Mama about it. Mama says we need legal representation urgently.

Lizzie

P.S. – What is the news of your uncle? Is he still in danger?

Dear Lizzie,

This is a terrible situation! I am as perplexed and distressed as you are. Of course I know your family are not to blame in this but no one is listening to me!

The accusation came from Meecham, of course.

Uncle is alive and is being cared for, but has not yet regained consciousness.

I have entreated with Aunt Betty for us to visit you at home, but she says that we are not to do so.

I am so sorry about Kofi! How can this be happening? I am doing my best to get to the truth.

Belle

Dear Belle,

Things have gone from bad to worse. After hours and hours of questioning by Meecham and his men, Joshua has been arrested!

We are all distraught. You can only imagine how Frances is feeling.

Meecham had the cheek to come here and say that Joshua delivered poisoned peppermint tea to your family. He said it was in the hamper that Mama sent with you after the meeting here that night! He says that Joshua has been spying on your family for the Sons and Daughters of Africa all along.

Meecham told us that your uncle was helping the Bow Street Runners to ambush the Sons and Daughters of Africa on their rescue missions! He says that that is the motive for the poisoning.

Belle – this is serious. Is there any chance this is true?

People are telling my family that if so, you and I cannot see each other again.

Can your uncle have betrayed us, Belle?

Lizzie

I sank down on to my bed, clutching Lizzie's letter. Now Joshua had been arrested!

I thought about that evening when he had driven me back from Sancho's after the meeting. His kindness to me, his gentle words of advice. I couldn't bear the thought of him behind bars. It was simply not possible he had poisoned Uncle. Was it?

And surely Uncle was not behind the ambushes on the Sons and Daughters of Africa? Meg and her crew had rescued me and Lizzie just a few months ago. Uncle had helped them out then and had been building a friendship with Mr Sancho ever since. He wanted slavery over and done with – he had said so! Why would he turn against the Sons and Daughters all of a sudden?

Meecham was lying, of that I was certain. But what damage might his lies do while I was trying to prove it? Even Lizzie had doubted Uncle. And with Uncle so ill, how would I get Joshua out of prison? Mr Knight had legal experience, but when Meecham had accused the Sanchos, Knight had been quick to assume their guilt. He wouldn't be the right person to help them at all!

Lizzie and I could not even see each other to work together on this.

And Kofi was still stuck at Hartmoor Hall.

Our world was descending into chaos.

ABOLITIONIST NEWS

SANCHOS TARGETED IN LATEST BOW STREET RUNNER ATTACK – MANSFIELD ILL, RECAPTURES SOAR

SANCHO'S TEA ROOM HAS BEEN TARGETED BY THE BOW STREET RUNNERS IN THE LATEST OF A SERIES OF AMBUSHES AND ATTACKS. OFFICERS TURNED OVER THE SDOA MEETING PLACE, CAUSING MANY POUNDS' WORTH OF DAMAGE, WHILE CLAIMING LINKS TO THE POISONING OF LORD MANSFIELD.

THE SANCHOS SAY THEY HAVE NO KNOWLEDGE OF THE ORIGINS OF THE POISON AND ARE URGING THEIR COMRADES TO BEWARE OF FALSE ACCUSATIONS.

MEANWHILE, SINCE LORD MANSFIELD HAS BEEN TAKEN ILL AT HIS LONDON HOME, SO-CALLED 'MASTERS' HAVE BEEN ACTING WITHOUT FEAR OF RECRIMINATION, SNATCHING PEOPLE FROM THE STREETS ONCE MORE IN A SURGE OF CLAIMS OF OWNERSHIP.

FREEDOM SEEKERS – BE VIGILANT!

Chapter Thirty-Three

That night I slept fitfully, my dreams wracked with visions of Uncle in his sick bed, Kofi trapped inside Hartmoor Hall, Joshua behind bars at Newgate.

And Lizzie, seen from a distance, walking further and further away from me.

The following morning I awoke early. I would have to do what I could alone. The only way to exonerate Joshua was to work out who the real poisoner was.

I myself had delivered that peppermint tea to Uncle that evening. Had I really passed on something to him that was laced with poison? Now Uncle was suffering from acute nausea and vomiting, and a loss of appetite, but neither Dr Simpson nor Meecham had been able to name the poison causing it. If I could identify the poison, might that help to pinpoint the poisoner?

I decided to start in the library. Within half an hour I had found the reference books I needed:

One Man's Meat – A Field Guide to Poisons
Poisonous Plants – A Beginner's Guide
The Kitchen Garden – A Botanical Bible

I trawled through each, scanning the pages for poisons that produced the effects that Uncle was suffering from. Noting the symptoms that tallied with Uncle's own, my search resulted in three possible options.

CASE NOTES – poisons and their effects

Deadly nightshade (Atropa belladonna)

Purple-green bell-shaped flowers. The green berries of the deadly nightshade ripen to black and are especially poisonous, causing **sweating, vomiting,** breathing difficulties, confusion, potential coma and death. Drops of belladonna ('beautiful woman') were used in ancient Greece by women to make their eyes appear larger.

Foxglove or folk's glove or dead man's bells (Digitalis purpurea)

Foxglove – used to treat dropsy (a failure of the heart) by slowing down the heart rate and enabling more blood to be pumped through the ventricles. The plant is extremely poisonous and should only be administered by a skilled healer. The juices of the petals, stem and leaves are all toxic. Can cause **nausea, vomiting,** dizziness, visual disturbances and cardiac irregularities or palpitations.

The name 'foxglove' was once thought to originate from a belief that foxes wore the bell flowers on their feet to silence their steps when out hunting.

Monkshood (Aconitum napellus)

A poisonous plant whose hooded blue flowers (also sometimes pink, yellow and white) grow on tall spikes. The roots are especially poisonous, causing **stomach pains and dizziness** if ingested. Fatal in large amounts, its unpleasant flavour means poisonings are rare. Can also affect the heart.

Also known as Adam and Eve or Devil's helmet.

Any of these could have been used to poison Uncle.

How would I narrow it down?

I ran over the symptoms again. While all of these poisons caused sickness and stomach pains, each had other symptoms too. Dr Simpson hadn't mentioned any visual disturbances, for example. Or breathing difficulties, for that matter. Monkshood seemed unlikely as Uncle would surely have noticed the taste.

I decided to walk among the plants in the Kenwood gardens and see what they could offer me. The gardens had been designed as a space of rest and relaxation. A place to soothe the mind, bring fresh air to the body and ease the spirit. To bring clarity to one's thoughts.

In the herb garden, the lavender bushes gave up their sweet floral perfume: calming, soothing, balancing. I thought of that day in the tea shop when I had first met Aja. She had spoken then of healing and of hurt. Lavender, chamomile, peppermint: these were plants with healing properties.

I could see Mrs Sancho now, scooping chamomile tea into a paper bag, twisting closed the top, handing it to me with her gap-toothed smile. Lizzie's mother was not capable of poisoning.

I crouched down and read the label marking the chamomile flowers.

Chamomile / Anthemis nobilis

Were there other plants growing elsewhere in the garden that had different kinds of power? Poisonous powers even, like those I had been reading of?

Carefully, I stepped through the ordered rows, taking in the beauty of the plants and flowers around me, stopping to read their labels.

At the southernmost end of the garden, in a soil border close to the wall, was a row of stems covered with pink and purple bells. Taking care not to touch them, I inhaled the scent from one of the heads. I was hit with a bitter, acrid smell, and I was instantly transported back to that night we tried to rescue Kofi. Of course! These were the flowers I had seen and smelled at Hartmoor Hall!

I bent to read the label:

Foxglove / Digitalis purpurea

So it was foxgloves that were growing in abundance at Hartmoor Hall! And where had I seen the word 'digitalis' before? I closed my eyes and imagined myself back in the garden. We had gone from there into the kitchen, and – yes! The jars in the kitchen we had seen had been labelled 'digitalis'.

That kitchen was not a garden kitchen, but a poison lab!

Was that where the poison used to lace the tea had come from?

Was Hugh Hartmoor Uncle's poisoner?

Chapter Thirty-Four

Was I reaching too far?

I knew Hartmoor to be a cruel man, who wanted above everything to protect his property, to protect what he saw as his right to mastery over others. In this respect he certainly had motive. Uncle's Somerset ruling pulled against the idea of people as property and Hartmoor and his son had openly expressed their fury and resentment at the money they had lost when the people they had enslaved sought their freedom.

But how would Hartmoor have even reached Uncle in the last couple of days? Uncle had not left the house in that time and Hartmoor had not been here at Kenwood.

Hartmoor had motive, but not opportunity.

I returned to the library and pulled out my notes on foxglove / digitalis and its symptoms, spreading the pages out on Uncle's desk. Uncle always recommended reviewing your thoughts again and again in the light of new information. *Nausea, vomiting, dizziness and cardiac irregularities.*

Uncle had complained days ago of trouble with his chest, and Aunt Betty had expressed fears about his heart. She had mentioned 'palpitations', putting them down to the stress of his work. Was it possible that those palpitations had been caused by foxglove poisoning?

I sat down and sketched out a timeline of the relevant events:

- Sunday 20 July – portrait stolen
- Monday 21 July – Uncle complains of palpitations
- Monday 21 July evening – Hamper from Sancho's to Uncle and Mr Knight with peppermint tea
- Friday 25 July – Chamomile tea from Mrs Sancho
- Sunday 27 July – Uncle takes sick, Dr Simpson visits and diagnoses poisoning

Unless I was missing something, the poison couldn't be responsible for Uncle's palpitations as he hadn't taken it yet.

If, that is, the poison was present in the tea from Sancho's. Which I didn't believe it was.

So where did that leave me?

I tried again.

- *Sunday 20 July – portrait stolen*
  Poison administered?
- *Monday 21 July – Uncle complains of palpitations*
- *Monday 21 July (evening) – Hamper from Sancho's to Uncle and Mr Knight with peppermint tea*
- *Friday 25 July – Chamomile tea from Mrs Sancho*
- *Sunday 27 July – Uncle takes sick, Dr Simpson visits and diagnoses poisoning*

So what if the poison *was* foxglove – digitalis – and what if it *had* caused Uncle's palpitations after all? That would mean it *wasn't* the peppermint tea from Sancho's that was poisoned – it had to be something Uncle had eaten or drunk prior to that!

And that would mean that the poison was never present in the tea from Sancho's – just as I had known in my gut all along.

So why had Meecham claimed that the Sancho's tea was the source of the poison? An error? Was he misled? Or was he just lying? We only had Meecham's word for it,

and I knew I didn't trust him. Meecham clearly had it in for the Sanchos and for the Sons and Daughters of Africa. It would suit him very well to be able to pin Uncle's poisoning on them.

If Uncle had been poisoned with digitalis, the poison had to have been given to him earlier – around the time the portrait had been stolen.

And that changed everything.

Dear Lizzie,

How are you all?

I am making good progress with the poison investigations. I hope to lift suspicion from your family and eliminate you all from the enquiries as soon as possible!

I believe that the poison given to Uncle may have been 'digitalis', an infusion made from distilled foxglove leaves. The leaves, petals and stems of the foxglove flower are all highly toxic – AND it was growing in abundance at Hartmoor Hall.

I am just trying to work out WHEN it may have first been administered.

On the note of motive, I believe that Hugh Hartmoor is the HH behind some malevolent letters written to the newspapers about Uncle and my presence here at Kenwood House. He has motive enough to harm Uncle but I cannot identify any opportunity.

If he is the poisoner, how would he have administered the poison?

Please keep in touch,
Belle

P.S. Regarding legal assistance, try Granville Sharp or Francis Hargrave.

A letter arrived from Lizzie later that same day.

Dear Belle,

For your urgent attention!

There was a newspaper clipping attached:

YOUNG LAW STUDENT MISSING

Law student Mr James Knight of Bristol has been reported missing from his home. He was last seen leaving to meet a friend from university, a fellow student in law, in London on Friday 18th July. Local magistrates are concerned for his safety.

Mr Knight, missing? Was he on the run perhaps?

A strange sensation crept over me.

If I was right about the possible timing of the digitalis poisoning . . . Well, it was immediately after Mr Knight's arrival that Uncle had begun to get sick! But then, what possible reason could Mr Knight have for wanting to harm

Uncle? They worked together, and he was a friend of the family. Uncle was helping him further his career and he was learning from Uncle about the law. He may have had opportunity, but what was his motive?

'Belle?'

I spun around. Mr Knight was standing in the library doorway.

The notes and clipping dropped from my hands and drifted impossibly slowly to the floor between us.

'Here, let me help you . . .'

Mr Knight knelt down and reached for one of the pages. Lizzie's letter, with the news clipping attached! I sprang forward and snatched up the page from the floor before he could touch it, swiftly gathered up the remaining notes and diagrams as he watched, bemused.

'I've been illustrating flowers and writing poetry,' I said breathlessly. 'To take my mind off things.'

'Wonderful!' he said, smiling. 'May I see?' He reached out his hand.

I stood up on wobbly legs. 'I'm still practising,' I said with a dismissive laugh, returning to the desk and replacing the drawings and notes in my pouch. How much had he seen? 'I fear my work is not yet ready to share.'

'What a shame,' he said coolly.

I turned back to him, the pouch of notes on the desk

behind me. There was an awkward silence. I forced a smile. It felt like my face was cracking open.

'You must be terribly worried about your uncle,' he said, with a sympathetic frown.

I nodded.

'Well,' he said brightly, turning to go. 'I've checked in on him and I'm going out for the day now. I have business to attend to in town. On your uncle's behalf of course.'

I nodded, wanting to speak, unable to find my voice.

'Your aunt's upstairs. Maybe you could help her attend to him?' He seemed unperturbed.

'Of course, Mr Knight.'

He paused at the door and turned back. 'It will be all right, you know, Belle,' he said, his voice earnest, reassuring. He watched me silently for a moment, then pulled a quick smile. 'Everything will work out just as it should.'

And with that, he left the room, pulling the door closed behind him.

Chapter Thirty-Five

I waited until I heard the front door close, then raced up to Uncle's room and threw the door open so hard it clattered against the wall.

Uncle was fast asleep and Aunt Betty was sitting in an armchair beside the bed, pulling a needle and thread through a cushion cover.

'Belle! You gave me quite a turn!' gasped my aunt. Uncle didn't stir but his chest rose and fell with a steady rhythm.

'Aunt Betty,' I said fervently. 'When are you expecting Mr Knight back?'

She shrugged. 'Not until this evening. He's out for the day, says he has business to attend to in town.'

'And you'll be here until then? Right here? With Uncle?'

Hearing the note of panic in my voice, she looked up. 'Of course I will, Belle.' She laid her sewing in her lap.

'Dear girl, whatever is the matter?'

I steeled myself. I couldn't tell her. Not yet. Not until I was certain. 'I have to go out, Aunt,' I said instead. 'I'll be back this afternoon. But in the meantime, please don't leave Uncle's side. And . . . and don't let anyone answer the door.'

'Dear girl, what on earth –'

I ran down to the laundry, and sifted through the neatly folded piles of clothing that the maids wore while they were working. I took a bonnet and an apron belonging to Nancy and hid them under my cloak. Then I changed into a pair of boots and set off.

The Spaniards Inn was a notorious place on Hampstead Lane for highwaymen, due to the way the road narrowed dangerously in front of it, to a point too pinched to allow two carriages to pass each other at the same time. Instead, each was forced to stop and agree who should pass first. Meanwhile, in the long grasses by the side of the road, professional cutpurses, pickpockets and highwaymen lay in wait, ready to swoop down on the unsuspecting travellers and hold them to ransom and gunpoint for their valuables.

Consequently, the inn had become a favourite stopping

point for such 'adventurers', who were always welcome by its fire. The landlord, Ned, had a reputation for his gruff but generous hospitality.

How I wished Lizzie were with me right now. But I had no choice but to press on alone. Reluctantly, I pushed open the door. A fire roared and danced in the grate. Two bearded men sat in the corner playing dice, and at another table a group of women huddled together, deep in conversation. Heads lifted as I entered. A serving girl in a fitted black dress and bodice moved from table to table. On one hand, she skilfully balanced a tray, from which she distributed silver tankards overspilling with frothy ale.

I nodded politely as I passed through the room and curtsied to the large, aproned man behind the bar. Ned, no doubt. His black hair was shorn close to his head, his face half obscured by a large black beard. He leaned on the counter on crossed arms and focused his steely blue eyes on me.

'What can I do for you, missy?' He spoke in the same Scottish tones as Uncle. I found it strangely comforting.

'I have an urgent message for Mr Knight,' I said, trying to keep the heiress out of my voice. 'I understand that he's staying here.'

'That he is,' said Ned. 'And what's your business with him?'

'I work up at Kenwood House, for the Mansfield family.'
I hated to tell a lie, but strictly speaking, in some senses,
this was not one.

The room fell silent. All eyes were on me. I had no
choice but to go on. 'Mr Knight has been conducting some
work there. I have an urgent message for him from Lady
Mansfield.'

Ned's heavy black eyebrows shot up. 'From the house,
you say?' This, said like an announcement to the room.

'Yes,' I said, looking about me. Did he not believe me?

He considered for a moment, then pulled out a cloth and
began to run it over the counter with vigour. 'He's staying
in the Oak Room, but he's not here presently.' He nodded
towards the fireplace. 'You're welcome to wait by the fire.
There's game pie in the oven. He'll be back in an hour or
so.'

An hour? That was plenty of time to check out his room
and see what I could find. I politely declined the meal but
said that yes, thank you, I would wait for his arrival. I added
that as it was a matter of some urgency I would wait outside
so as to catch him as soon as he returned.

'As you wish,' Ned conceded, turning to a waiting
customer.

Outside, I slipped around to the back of the building and
re-entered the inn through the rear door. The guests in the

bar had resumed their conversations; someone was singing. I snuck up the stairs and took the corridor on the first floor, scanning the doors until I found the Oak Room.

The door was locked.

I felt under my cap for a hairpin and pulled one from my hair. I was familiar with the practice of lockpicking from my readings of court cases rather than through any practical experience, but it was worth a try at least. I bent down in front of the door, passed the pin into the keyhole and tried to hook the lock from inside. I twisted the pin slowly in different directions until I heard a distinct click from inside the keyhole. I turned the doorknob. It gave to the right and the door opened. Wait until I told Lizzie about that!

The room was set with a bed on one side and a small wooden writing desk on the other. On the desk were a pile of clean papers and a box of writing materials: quill pens, a bottle of ink, a tablet of wax for sealing letters. The tablet bore the imprints of a signet ring that had been pressed into the wax many times, but the shapes overlapped and melded into one another and it was impossible to discern the shape of the seal.

In the centre of the desk lay an invitation:

I staggered back with the invitation in my hand and slumped on to the bed. I had to read it again for it to make sense.

Was Mr Knight a member of the Brotherhood of Masters, invited to the unveiling of the Hartmoors' portrait? How could he be a member of the Brotherhood and be working on runaway cases with Uncle? It made no sense at all! And surely Aunt and Uncle would not invite such a person to be so close to them, to work with Uncle even?

But the unveiling of the portrait of Hartmoor and

his son was planned for tonight. Did this mean that Mr Gainsborough had painted Kofi into the portrait after all? As soon as I left here, I would get word to Lizzie to meet me at Hartmoor Hall with the Sons and Daughters of Africa. We would attend the unveiling ourselves.

I shoved the invitation into the pocket of my apron and opened the desk drawer. Inside was a mess of papers and newspaper clippings.

Suddenly, I heard the tread of footsteps coming up the corridor. I froze. They passed. Breathing more easily, I spread the pile of papers out on the desk. Among them were two newspaper clippings:

YOUNG LAW STUDENT MISSING

Law student Mr James Knight of Bristol has been reported missing from his home. He was last seen leaving to meet a friend from university, a fellow student in law, in London on Friday 18th July. Local magistrates are concerned for his safety.

This was the clipping Lizzie had sent me! The second read:

Mr James Knight, law student, has been found poisoned in his room in an inn in Deptford. Mr Knight had been missing for some weeks after meeting with an old friend from university. At first it was believed that Mr Knight had died of natural causes – heart palpitations. However, closer inspection of the body revealed digitalis poisoning in his system. Local magistrates are urging anyone to come forward who may have information pertaining to Mr Knight's murder.

Terror seized every fibre of my body.

If Mr James Knight, law student, was dead – poisoned! – then who was the man who had been coming to our house each day for the last fortnight?

Chapter Thirty-Six

My hands began to tremble uncontrollably. My legs lost all their strength.

However much I disliked the man I had believed to be Mr Knight, however uncomfortable he had made me feel, I had relied on the knowledge that he was a friend of the family, and therefore a friend *to* the family. If this man was not who he said he was, he could be anybody!

Suddenly I was gripped by an icy fear. Digitalis . . . Was this man, who had spent so much time in our home, the person who had poisoned the real James Knight? If so, did that mean . . .

I had to get back to Kenwood! But first I needed evidence of who this man might be and what he was up to. I scanned the room again. Aside from the desk, there was not much to see. I reached inside the desk drawer once more and felt around. My fingers lighted on something small, metal, heavy.

It was a signet ring, the kind used to seal letters in wax.

A sickly cold suspicion stole over me.

If I was right, the ring would confirm it. I took it from the drawer with shaking fingers – but it slipped away from me, hit the floor and rolled under the desk. No!

I fell to my knees and looked underneath the desk. I needed to find that ring! It was a crucial piece of evidence. If he were to come back and find it gone, he would know that I – or someone – had been in here. And what would he do then?

I could not see the ring anywhere. I reached under the desk and ran my fingers along the floorboards. Between two of the boards, a hole. It must have dropped through! Desperate, I stood up and shoved the desk aside. Heavier than it looked, it resisted the force of my push and scraped noisily along the floor.

There was the ring, between the floorboards! It seemed to wink at me in the dying light. But the hole was too small for my hand to fit through.

I looked around the room wildly. I needed something, anything, to help me get the ring out. Some kind of hook, a piece of metal wire. I put my hand to my head and drew out another hairpin. The coils on one side of my head fell to my shoulder. The pin was about four inches long, with a small hook on the end. It was perfect.

I lay down on my stomach and slowly poked the hooked end of the pin through the hole. My breath came thick and fast. My hand trembled. I jabbed it at the ring, which in turn spun an inch away from me. I took a deep breath. I had to get this right.

Footsteps, coming up the corridor. Was it him coming back?

I closed my eyes and took three breaths in and out to steady my nerves and still my chattering mind. Slowly this time, with precision, I lowered the hairpin into the hole. Missed. Tried again. The hook slipped into the ring's O. I lifted it gently – and the ring came with it.

Outside the door, the footsteps drew closer.

I clambered to my feet, clutching my trophy. Then I held it up to the window to see the shape engraved on its flat surface. A dark gold colour, it flashed and glinted at me in the late-afternoon sunlight. The shape engraved at its centre was as clear as day – and confirmed my worst fears.

It was the head of a stag.

My blood chilled and slowed in my veins. I pulled the invitation out of my pocket and read it again.

Sir Hugh Hartmoor MP, planter, botanist, physician, collector, West India Merchant and Master and his son Rupert Hartmoor, student in law and heir to the Hartmoor estate . . .

All the breath went out of me.

The footsteps stopped outside the door.

I slipped the ring into my pocket and took a step back as the doorknob turned slowly and the door swung open on its hinges. There in the doorway, in his sky-blue frockcoat, holding the key in his grey-gloved hands, stood the man I had believed until now to be James Knight – Rupert Hartmoor.

Chapter Thirty-Seven

Clearly unsurprised to see me there, he cast his eyes over the room.

'What are you doing in my room, Belle?' he inquired.

Feigning relief at his arrival had to be worth a shot. I couldn't let him know that I now knew who he was. I had to buy some time to think.

'Mr Knight!' I gasped, feigning relief. 'Thank goodness you're here! I was looking for you.'

He stepped in and closed the door behind him. My hand closed around the pin in my pocket. He began to walk the edges of the room, surveying it for signs of disturbance.

'I mean,' I stammered, 'I was waiting for you.'

He paused at the desk, now at an odd angle a foot or so away from its original position. He glanced down at the hole in the floorboards.

'The landlord said I could wait up here.' The silence was excruciating. 'Someone was cleaning the room . . . the door was open.' The brightness of my voice was brittle as bone china.

'I see.' He walked a slow circle around me. I swallowed hard, tried not to tremble. 'And what can I do for you?'

'Uncle's taken a turn for the worse. I . . . . I thought perhaps you could help. I didn't know where else to go –'

Hartmoor's eyes glinted. 'A turn for the worse? So he is . . . dangerously ill?'

A cat now, toying with its mouse. He opened the desk drawer and looked inside as I slowly forced breath into my lungs and out again. He slid it shut again without a word, then faced me.

'In that case he must be attended to as a matter of urgency.' He spread his arms as though it were a simple explanation of the obvious. 'I will take him to a physician I know well. He is very skilled in these matters.' He kept his gaze on my face, as though trying to read me while I read him. 'He has extensive experience of dealing with poisons.'

My face betrayed not a trace of my crumbling nerves.

He turned towards the door. 'Then it's straight to Kenwood to collect your uncle now! I've got the carriage. I'll take your aunt Betty with me too.'

He had absolutely no intention of taking Aunt and Uncle to a doctor, I knew that much. So what was his plan? Did he intend to take us to Hartmoor Hall? Much as I hated the thought of returning to that horrible place, I knew that this was my only chance of exposing Rupert Hartmoor and his father in public for who they really were. The portrait was due to be unveiled there in just a few hours.

And, so long as I was with Aunt and Uncle, I could do all in my power to protect them.

'Thank you,' I said breathlessly, moving to leave with him.

'Oh, no, no, no!' he said as he opened the door. Turning back, he flashed those too-white teeth at me for an instant in cold mimicry of a smile. 'I think it's best you stay here.'

My heart plummeted. Of course. He knew exactly what I was up to. Knew that his deception had been discovered. How long had he known, I wondered?

I glanced towards the door, desperately trying to imagine my next move.

'Oh, and don't bother screaming for help,' he added. 'I've warned them downstairs that you might. I've told them that they are to ignore you, no matter what you say.' His eyes narrowed sharply. 'That you are a petty thief who has stolen from me, and that you are to be kept here until the Bow Street Runners arrive.'

He stepped out into the corridor and closed the door between us, leaving me alone with the sound of the key turning in the lock with a decisive click.

Chapter Thirty-Eight

I ran to the door and pulled the hairpin from my pocket. I thrust it into the keyhole as I had before, but my fingers were thick and rubbery with fear, and I couldn't seem to make any contact inside the lock. I took a breath and tried again. And again, and again. But the pin, slippery between my fingers, just kept twisting around and around.

Hot tears of frustration sprang to my eyes. But this was no time to feel defeated. I had to think and act fast.

I banged on the door and shouted for help, but downstairs the crowd were still singing to their hearts' content. I could not be heard. I ran to the window and opened it, but I was two floors up. If I jumped I would be sure to break bones.

I thought of the hole I had seen in the floorboards. Was there any chance of breaking through the floor into the room below? I dropped to the floor, wiggled my fingers through the gap as far as I could, gripped the floorboard and pulled. It creaked and strained, but held fast.

I got to my feet, crouching now to gain some leverage from my legs, and tried again. This time the board broke free and I tumbled backwards on to the floor, the floorboard broken clean away in my hand. I went to take another – and saw, in the gap that I had made in the floor, the image of my own face staring back at me. From canvas.

Was it possible?

I grasped a second board, ripped it free.

Miss Harry's portrait of our families! It was under the floorboards, here in Hartmoor's room! Was he the person who had broken it out of the library then? And yet he was still at the house just after the theft. He had joined us for the discussion with Meecham. How was that possible?

Someone hammered on the door. 'Is anyone in there?'

I ran to it. 'Yes! Yes, I'm locked in! Can you –'

The sound of the lock rattling – the door was flung open. It was Ned, his face like thunder. 'So that blaggard locked you in here!'

I was confused. Was he letting me go? Tears were threatening but I fought them down. 'He said no one would come! He said you would keep me here!'

'Oh, I was coming!' said Ned grimly. 'That one's not paid a penny of his bill yet, so I don't owe him any favours!

Don't know who he thinks he is, ordering everyone about the place like we work for him!' Here he looked rather sheepish. 'Plus, I don't want the Bow Street Runners up here in my business what with the nature of my . . . clientele. Wanted sorts, you understand. Come on, lass . . .'

He glanced at the floor, saw a glimpse of the painting, then back at me.

'Oh, you found it then! I didn't bat an eyelid when he rocked up here with it last week. We see all sorts, you understand. And then he cleared off again sharpish. Was in and out within minutes.' He cleared his throat. 'I'm glad you found it, though. Just as well. There were some downstairs that had their eye on having it off him and selling it.'

Downstairs in the tavern, the customers quietened as we entered.

'Do you think you could lend me a horse, please?' I asked, leaning on the counter for support. My head was swimming. 'Only, he's taken my aunt and uncle, and I need to hurry –'

'Your aunt and uncle?' Ned said sharply. 'At Kenwood House? I thought you said you worked for them.'

It was too late. I had already made the error. Cowed, I nodded.

'So you *are* Miss Dido Belle,' he said quietly.

Faces turned towards me from the bar, from the tables.

A dark-haired man reluctantly slid a coin across a table to his jet-haired female companion, who proudly tucked it into the shoulder of her dress.

'I'm sorry I lied,' I said, addressing the room, more than a little abashed. 'But my family are in terrible danger. Please can you help me?'

The old man sitting in the corner got to his feet and pulled his pipe from his mouth. 'Your aunt and uncle host meals for us every year, so they do!' he said, looking around at the other faces in the room. 'Every Harvest, Every Christmas. Far as we're concerned, they're decent people.'

Ned nodded in agreement. 'Tell us what you need, Miss Belle,' he ordered, bringing his fist down on the counter. 'And it'll be done.'

Dusk was falling fast. Rupert Hartmoor had taken Aunt and Uncle to Hartmoor Hall, I was certain of it. But what did he have planned for them? That didn't bear thinking about.

First, I needed to send a message to Lizzie to tell her to get to Hartmoor Hall immediately. The unveiling of the portrait was due to take place there at eight o'clock.

That gave us just a couple of hours to gather as many people together as possible. Meg would need to drum up support from whoever was left of the Sons and Daughters of Africa. If members of Hartmoor's Brotherhood were going to be present at the unveiling, we would need all the numbers we could muster.

Sam, the inn's ostler, and Lily, his daughter, offered to ride into town to give my messages to Lizzie and Meg. I imagined Lily was only a year or so younger than me. She smiled and gave me a shy wave as they left.

Ned lent me a horse from the Spaniards Inn stables so that I did not have to break my journey at Kenwood. A tough grey mare named Minerva, she was a larger, heavier animal than I was used to, but she was strong. Speed was of the essence, and Ned assured me that she could get me to Hartmoor Hall within the half hour. He gave me directions, wished me luck, and sent me on my way.

I rode north from Hampstead, past Finchley, and up towards the woods that harboured Hartmoor Hall. Once more, the houses fell back behind me as the sun set. Once more, the evening music of the countryside folded me into its embrace: the woody chirruping of crickets, the lonely cry of an owl.

I turned off the main road down the woodland path. Hartmoor Hall loomed into view on the horizon, a great grey shadow cast in stone against the doleful sky. On seeing its towers and turrets again, I quailed momentarily. Had the house been designed to inspire dread?

I steered Minerva into the trees and slowed our pace. Then I jumped down from her back, tied her to the tree by the stream, and waited for the others to arrive.

Before long, I heard the sound of hooves tramping through the undergrowth. Between the trees, just ahead, the golden glow of a lit lantern. Then another and another. Small groups of men and women moved into view on either side of the path, gathered in clusters around single lanterns. Sons and Daughters of Africa. Dozens of them!

'Belle!'

Lizzie ran out of the woods and threw her arms around me. It had been days since we had seen each other – days since the Hartmoors' poisonous dealings had got in between us! I could have cried with relief but for now I held back my tears.

Lizzie held me firmly by the shoulders, her features agitated. 'When I saw that the real Mr Knight was missing, I was so worried! But the Bow Street Runners were guarding the shop. I couldn't even get out to meet you –'

'Knight is Hartmoor!' I burst out.

Lizzie looked shocked. 'What?'

'He's the Stag's son – I mean, Hugh Hartmoor's son – Rupert!'

Lizzie's eyes widened. 'You mean Hartmoor's son has been at your house all that time?'

The horror of it gripped me all over again. 'And,' I whispered, pulling everything together, 'he's the man that shot at us that night . . .'

A woman stepped out of the trees, pushed her hood back off her head and shook out her braids. Aja.

'I've come to help,' she said.

Meg emerged from the shadows. 'I didn't want her to go in there,' she said, indicating the house with a perfunctory nod. 'But she insists.'

'I have unfinished business with the Hartmoors,' Aja said, her eyes locked on the house. 'It's time.'

'They've got my aunt and uncle in there too,' I said, feeling weak with relief that everyone was here. 'I think they're planning something awful.'

'Then let's get going,' said Meg. 'The Sons and Daughters will form a ring of protection around the house. Those men won't be going anywhere unless we say so.'

'How did you gather so many people together?' I whispered to Lizzie as we stole towards the house. 'What about all the arrests?'

'I followed up the lawyer leads you gave me,'

Lizzie said, keeping her eyes on the house as we moved through the undergrowth. 'Granville Sharp, Francis Savage. They managed to free Joshua and they've been working through each case. Once Joshua was free, he was able to help with the other cases too. There's still much to do, but we're getting there.'

Silently, Meg directed two young women towards the back of the house. They edged their way along the side wall in the darkness and disappeared into the garden. Staying low, Lizzie and I crept up to the front entrance and stood either side of the central dining-room window, pressing ourselves against the wall. I peeped inside.

Hugh Hartmoor's hulking figure passed across the window, making me flinch back. Aunt Betty was seated at the table, her back to us. Stretched out on a chaise longue on the other side of the room, clutching his stomach, was Uncle William.

I turned in desperation to Aja, who had hung back with us. 'Do you think we're too late to save Uncle? He looks so unwell . . .'

But Aja was transfixed by something – or rather some*one* – in the room. Moving around the table, pouring wine from a large flagon into Hartmoor's glass.

Kofi.

Aja stared and stared. Her hand went up to her mouth.

Her eyes filled with tears. She had found who she had come for. She had found her son. She took in a long breath, exhaled slowly, squared her shoulders.

'Right,' she said, pulling a pistol from the belt slung around her middle. 'We're going in.'

Chapter Thirty-Nine

The plan was that Meg and Aja would enter the dining room by the ground-floor door. Armed with pistols, they would cover that door so the Hartmoors had no chance of escape. Lizzie and I, along with a cohort of Daughters of Africa, would occupy the balcony above. From there we could stop the portrait viewing, challenge the Hartmoors and ensure that our story was heard in full, with witnesses. Brother Cugoano was stationed at the entrance to the wood, waiting for Frances and Joshua to arrive with Mr and Mrs Sancho.

We crept along the balcony and took up our position, crouched on the floor, looking down on the dining room.

Against the end wall, below the stag's head, stood an easel supporting a canvas draped with a green velvet curtain. Hugh Hartmoor stood at the head of the table, in a too-tight scarlet frockcoat, hands clasped behind his back, moving his weight backwards and forwards over his heels. His cheeks were more reddened than usual and he surveyed the room with bloodshot eyes.

His son Rupert leaned against the far wall, pulling at his gloved fingers, his face a smooth mask. Was he missing his ring? I patted my pocket. This was a solid piece of evidence.

Looking at Rupert Hartmoor now, I could hardly believe it was the same man who had seemed so keen to work with Uncle. Now I wondered what he had been doing all that time in the library. Aunt Betty had spoken of Uncle's files going missing. Rupert Hartmoor was no doubt responsible – sabotaging Uncle's work on the runaway cases. Of course! That was why he had wormed his way into our home. Not only had Uncle made no progress since his arrival – things had got considerably worse. The numbers of so-called masters recapturing freedom seekers had soared. Ugly work indeed.

The dining room began to fill up with guests.

In came Meecham and two of his officers. Gainsborough and Dupont stood together in the corner of the room. Gainsborough looked nervously about him. Dupont kept his eyes on Meecham. This was the first we had seen of them since our last visit here. So they had gone ahead and added Mercury to the portrait after all? I felt a bitter stab of disappointment.

Next to them stood Miss Harry. What was she doing here? Hoping to confront the Hartmoors on her own behalf perhaps? I caught a shared glance between Miss Harry and Mr Gainsborough. Some kind of mutual acknowledgment. What did they know?

'Who are those others?' whispered Lizzie, indicating a small cluster of men in wide-skirted black frockcoats standing by the window in close formation, like a murder of crows.

'Artists?' I offered. 'I recognise them from our trip to the Academy.'

One of them threw a casual glance around the room. It was the skinny clerk who had thrown us out so unceremoniously. I nudged Lizzie and nodded towards the offending guest. Her eyes narrowed sharply at the sight of him.

Someone was tapping a fork on glass.

'Now then!' barked Hugh Hartmoor. 'Brothers and . . . others!'

The room tittered.

'Thank you all for coming!' he boomed pompously. 'You are about to see the unveiling of a portrait a long time in the making.' He threw a menacing look at Gainsborough.

The artist held his gaze unflinchingly. Something dark and unspoken crackled between them. Unbridled mutual hostility.

Hartmoor went on. 'An image of our past, present and future – preserving our power for posterity! I give you the latest work by one of the greatest artists of the age, the Hartmoor Portrait!'

He lifted the curtain with a flourish.

Beside me, Lizzie stifled a grin behind her hand. Someone coughed back a laugh. A gasp went up around the room.

The painting was not what any of us expected to see.

It was a portrait of Kofi and Kofi alone. Wearing a smart green coat and looking straight out at us with a defiant smile, a shiny red apple in his hand, from which he had taken a single bite. His skin was radiant with health; joy danced in his sparkling brown eyes.

The style was unmistakable.

It was by Miss Jane Harry.

How on earth . . .?

Miss Harry's face bore the faintest trace of a smile as she exchanged a nod of complicity with Mr Gainsborough. They must have arranged the switch between them!

Hugh Hartmoor stared open-mouthed at the painting as gasps became guffaws. Kofi hovered by the door, looking from Hugh Hartmoor to Rupert Hartmoor, his expression suspended somewhere between surprise and fear, poised as if to run.

Lizzie side-eyed me. 'Now!' she whispered urgently.

The two of us pushed up on to our feet and stood tall. Either side of us on the balcony, ten Daughters of Africa stepped out of the shadows as one.

The dozen or so faces in the dining room below suddenly looked up. Aunt Betty let out a little cry of surprise.

Hartmoor turned beetroot with rage. 'Meecham!' he thundered. 'Get up there, man!'

As Meecham made a move for the door, it burst open. There stood Meg and Aja, side by side, pistols cocked and ready. Meecham backed away, hands in the air. The two women strode across the threshold and moved slowly around the room, keeping their eyes – and their pistols – very firmly trained on Meecham and the men of the Brotherhood, who were now skittering backwards towards the far wall.

'What the devil's going on!' said Hartmoor through gritted teeth, standing his ground.

Aja approached Hartmoor, her gun pointed steadily at his chest. Defiantly, he drew himself up – but as she neared, his mouth fell open.

'You . . .' he whispered.

He shot a hasty look towards Kofi, finally understanding.

Kofi however remained rooted to the spot, He had not yet recognised his mother.

Aja tipped her chin and waved her gun for Hartmoor to join Rupert and the other men herded into the corner of the room. Without taking his enraged gaze off her, he slunk towards them.

In the doorway appeared Brother Cugoano, closely followed by Frances, Joshua and Mr and Mrs Sancho. Joshua! He strode over to stand guard over Hartmoor and the cowering Brotherhood. Frances and Mr Sancho sat down at the table on either side of Aunt Betty, who was pinned to her seat, looking dazed, fragile.

Mrs Sancho rushed to Uncle's side on the sofa. 'He needs water!' she said, her hand on his forehead.

Aunt Betty, finally finding the courage to stand, poured a glass and knelt down by Uncle, holding it to his lips. Aja produced a phial from her pocket and urged Uncle to drink its contents.

No one else moved.

'You will regret barging into my property!' raged Hartmoor, looking wildly about him. 'I'll have you thrown in jail, the lot of you!'

Meg threw up her hand to stop him. 'That's enough from you,' she ordered, casting her eyes up to the balcony.

I caught her eye and she gave me a solemn nod of encouragement.

'It's time for the girls to speak,' she declared.

Chapter Forty

I rested my hands on the edge of the balcony as I addressed the crowd below. At last the Hartmoors and their accomplice would be held to account.

'Some of you came to see a portrait unveiled this evening,' I announced, my voice quaking in spite of myself. 'I am glad to see that the portrait revealed was not the one you expected.'

Outraged mutters from the corner of the room downstairs mingled with murmurs of encouragement from the balcony.

'But some of us came here tonight to see justice done,' I continued, my voice growing bolder. 'And we will not be disappointed!'

'Hear hear!' said a voice from the floor. Sister Clara, one of the Daughters of Africa we had seen at the combat training.

'The house is surrounded!' declared Lizzie, moving along the balcony. She held herself tall, her hands clasped behind her back, walking with deliberate strides. I realised how like those Daughters of Africa she looked now. Would she be training to fight alongside them soon?

A few members of the Brotherhood glanced anxiously towards the windows. Others eyed the door.

'And you will hear us out!' Lizzie affirmed, nodding at me to continue.

I surveyed the room. The chandelier glittered cruelly, throwing eerie splinters of light on to the faces of the gathered crowd. 'There are several men in this room who have stains on their consciences,' I proclaimed, looking down at the Brotherhood, huddled in the corner of the room. 'Perhaps even blood on their hands.'

There was a drone of dissent. I lifted my hand to silence it. 'There are two men in particular here this evening, who have incarcerated a young boy against his will for weeks now, subjecting him to abominably cruel treatment.'

The Sons and Daughters murmured their dismay. Brother Cugoano extended a hand towards Kofi, drew him to his side.

'Someone else here has worked with them to plot against the life of my uncle, the Lord Chief Justice!'

I looked directly at Meecham as I said this. He swallowed and looked away.

Uncle sat up straighter now, but was gazing up at me, glassy and confused. Of course. I was still wearing Nancy's clothes, and my unpinned hair had fallen down about my shoulders.

'I will begin with the unveiling of a portrait at Kenwood,' I said. 'The Mansfield-Sancho Portrait by Miss Jane Harry.' Miss Harry placed her palms together in front of her and nodded up at me in a gesture of friendship and respect. 'Miss Harry's portrait showed both families as equal on the canvas. A harmonious vision of unity.'

Lizzie appeared in the lamplit spot at the other end of the balcony and took over the story. 'But the Mansfield-Sancho Portrait was stolen in a violent interruption of our celebrations.' Her voice carried steadily across the dining room. 'The theft of the portrait never really made any sense. It always seemed like a physical impossibility. Why *was* that? Meecham's –'

'INSPECTOR Meecham!' said Meecham feebly, straightening his coat.

Lizzie ignored him. 'Meecham's account of the theft told us that the painting had been stolen at around nine o'clock, the time at which we all heard the library window smash. Meecham claimed that while on guard outside the door, he heard the smash and entered the library just as the thief was jumping out of the window.'

There was a ripple of discontent among the Sons and Daughters at this. Meecham was looking around him uneasily and his forehead had broken out in a clammy sweat.

Lizzie was getting into her stride now. 'But the smashed glass was supposed to signify the thief's entry. Would anyone have had time to enter through the broken window, run to the painting, take it from the wall and get it out of the library window again, in the time it would have taken Meecham to simply open the door? Even with a key that jammed?'

'No way!' someone shouted from the gallery.

'And yet!' said Lizzie, spreading her arms wide. 'Meecham would have us believe it so!'

'Foul play for sure,' muttered Joshua, flint-eyed. To think that Meecham had arrested Joshua, thrown *him* behind bars. It was beyond belief.

The fire crackled and hissed ominously in the hearth, the flames throwing grotesque dancing shadows up the dark damask walls. The night wind whipped around in the chimney, sending out a mournful song.

I spoke again, this time with a bolder voice, clear as a bell. 'When we had to smash a window to get ourselves out of a tight spot the following day, we remembered that the shattered glass from the window was on the pathway outside the library, but there was virtually no glass on the library floor. Surely if the window had been broken from the outside, the glass would have fallen *in*?'

Hums and hahs of agreement floated up to me.

'Which suggests,' I concluded, 'that the glass was in fact broken from *inside* the library. Wasn't it, Meecham?'

Meecham planted his feet as though bracing himself. He lifted his chin, his nose twitched. 'Not necessarily!' he blustered.

'I should point out, ladies and gentlemen,' I added, archly, 'that while Meecham is here, he is not here on professional duties, but as a fully operational member of the Brotherhood of Masters. Isn't that so?'

Sweating profusely, Meecham tugged at his collar.

'Shame on you, Meecham!' shouted Miss Harry.

I continued. 'At eight o clock, after the speeches, everyone left the library to dance. Everyone except for Meecham and one of the guests, who later told us he was not much of a dancer.'

At this, bemused rumblings from the Sons and Daughters.

I spoke with purpose, to make sure everyone could hear. 'Meecham cleared the hall so that no one would witness him and the guest carrying the portrait out of the library, through the hall and out of the front door. That guest met with his accomplice – his father, in fact – and they took the painting in a carriage to his accommodation at the Spaniards Inn, where it has been hiding under the floorboards beneath his room ever since.'

'So the portrait is safe?' cried Miss Harry, her hands flying up to her face. 'Retrieved?'

'Indeed it is, Miss Harry,' I confirmed. 'And on its way back to Kenwood.'

Uncle was stirring. Aunt Betty was holding his hand and mopping at his brow with her handkerchief.

I walked along the balcony so that I was directly above them. 'After dropping the painting off in his room at the Spaniards Inn, the guest returned to the party as though nothing had happened. Meanwhile Meecham returned to the library, which was already devoid of the portrait. There, *he* smashed the window – from the inside, that is, foolishly spilling the glass on to the path – hoping to give everyone the impression that someone had just broken in. He jumped out and gave chase to an imaginary thief, for show!'

'Of course, no one suspected Meecham as his story was corroborated by his accomplice,' added Lizzie.

'Mr Knight?' said Aunt Betty, standing up suddenly. 'You mentioned the Spaniards Inn! Was it Mr *Knight* who stole the painting?'

Rupert Hartmoor was standing at the edge of the group of men in the corner, leaning on the window frame, smiling mirthlessly.

'So he would have had us believe, Aunt Betty,' I said. 'Yes, this man – who has been working with Uncle all this time – is the thief. But he is not James Knight! He impersonated his university friend James Knight, in order to infiltrate our family.'

With a trembling hand, I produced from the pocket of my dress the news clippings about the disappearance and subsequent poisoning of James Knight. The crowd listened in stunned silence while I read them aloud. Aunt Betty's face drained of colour.

'That man stole James Knight's identity to infiltrate our household, just hours before he stole the portrait on behalf of the Brotherhood of Masters. They didn't want a painting in the public realm that showed us on an equal footing with a family like the Sanchos. They didn't want people to see them looking dignified, independent, cultured, free. That man!' I pointed to Rupert Hartmoor, so that there could be no doubt as to his true identity. 'That man stole the painting, then returned to Kenwood to present himself as both a witness and a hero.'

Aunt Betty spoke up, her voice strained with despair. 'You mean that he is an impostor? And the *real* Mr James Knight is . . . dead?'

I nodded, my heart heavy for her. She turned away with a muted sob. I had to steady myself to carry on.

'What do you say to that, Mr Hartmoor?'

'Hartmoor?' whispered Uncle. This was the first word he had spoken. 'This man . . . is a *Hartmoor?*'

'Yes, Uncle,' I replied. 'Rupert Hartmoor. Pro-slavery lobbyist. Sir Hugh's son and heir to the Hartmoor fortune.'

Rupert Hartmoor said nothing.

'And there will be precious little left of that fortune, thanks to you, Mansfield!' said Hugh Hartmoor, belligerent as ever. 'Since your Somerset ruling, our fortunes dwindle by the day!'

'Ladies and gentlemen,' Lizzie announced sardonically. 'I give you – Hugh Hartmoor, Member of Parliament for Collingwood.'

Chapter Forty-One

'I'd like to tell you about Hugh Hartmoor,' said Aja now. 'I know him very well.'

Hugh Hartmoor's face tightened.

Aja swept a hand over the shiny reddish surface of the dining-room table. 'Mahogany,' she announced. 'Extracted from the island of Jamaica. Those beautiful majestic trees, cut down so that you could gorge yourselves at a fine mahogany table and then put your boots up on top of it!'

Hugh Hartmoor lunged towards Aja. Without turning her head, Sister Clara felled him with a single sideways chop of her right arm. He dropped to one knee, spluttering. The women stationed on the balcony took a step forward.

'This man bought me when I was just twelve years old, and set me to work alongside nearly two hundred men and women on his sugar plantation.' Aja's voice rang out around the silent room. 'There are no words for the cruelties he inflicted upon us. No human being should ever have to bear the like.'

No one spoke. A couple of the Sons and Daughters reached for each other's hands as they listened. Kofi stepped out of the shadows, watching Aja intently.

'We crafted our escape and started new lives. I married a man I loved, bore a child I loved.'

Kofi moved towards her as if in a dream.

'Letting you go was the hardest thing I have ever done,' she said, drawing him to her and running her hand gently over the roundness of his head. Her voice cracked as she spoke. 'But I believed that I was sending you to a life of freedom.' She shook her head slowly. 'Little did I know that slavery was alive and well on England's shore.'

'I have dreamed of you every night,' Kofi said slowly, gazing at his mother in wonder. 'Heard your voice singing to me! And now here you are, standing in front of me . . .'

He threw his arms around Aja's neck, buried his face in her shoulder. I swallowed the lump that rose in my throat. Grief at my own losses mingled with joy and relief for Kofi and his mother.

'How could I ever have imagined that the same man who had held me in captivity all those years ago would one day take my son?' Aja whispered, cradling Kofi in her arms.

Hartmoor staggered to his feet. 'You said yourself that you left him something to remember you by,' he snarled, eying the nearby Daughters of Africa warily. 'His eyes recalled yours when I saw him in the auction room. As soon as I saw the bracelet on his wrist, I knew he was your son. It seemed too good to be true. I would have paid any price to own the son of the woman who poisoned me.'

'I could have taken your life, Hartmoor!' cried Aja. 'And yet I chose to spare you! And not a day goes by when I do not regret my decision.'

'Well, he's mine now,' said Hartmoor bullishly.

Aja pushed Kofi behind her. 'He most certainly is not! Only the bonds of family deserve such expression! No human being can ever own another!' She looked up to the women who stood in the gallery. 'We are people, not property!'

'People not property!' they rejoined. 'People not property!'

The chorus of resistance rang out around the room. When it died down, Aja stepped towards Hartmoor and pushed her chin into the air.

'You are master over no one.'

Chapter Forty-Two

My eyes raked over the room we stood in. Everything about it spoke to the rancid power that Hartmoor had sought to wield over Kofi, over Aja, over us all. The stag heads glaring mutely from the walls, pitiful trophies of his urge to revel in taking life. The expensive deep green damask curtains at the window, moth-eaten and worn from lack of care. The dust and dirt that festered in the corners of a room that groaned under the weight of ill-gotten wealth.

Lizzie was watching Hartmoor through narrowed eyes, still smarting no doubt from his callous violence towards Kofi. Now she took over the telling once more.

'Hugh Hartmoor hated that anyone should have tried to claim their freedom from him,' she said. 'Lord Mansfield, when you passed the Somerset ruling in 1772, it encouraged more and more enslaved brothers and sisters to seek their freedom by running away. But as the Sons and Daughters of Africa will tell you, we have always resisted enslavement in so many ways!'

Applause went up from the balcony, accompanied by shouts of 'Hear! Hear!'

Lizzie reached into the pouch on her shoulder and pulled out a copy of *Abolitionist News*, thrusting it into the air. 'Rebellions in the Caribbean have been slavery's constant companion. Plantation fires, poisonings, uprisings. Whispers travel on the wind even between here and the islands.'

She paced the balcony as she continued to deliver her testimony. 'Hartmoor held Lord Mansfield personally responsible for the rise in people running away here in London. We heard that from his own lips! He began to put pressure on him to reverse the Somerset ruling by writing letters to him and to the newspapers.'

'I found one of those letters,' I confirmed, remembering the feeling of nausea it had given me. 'Ugly, harsh words. Poisonous thoughts about my presence at Kenwood. Hartmoor didn't think that I should be treated like a member of the family. He and his son plotted to infiltrate our family, to find ways to reverse Uncle's ruling, to undo his legal work on slavery, so that they could continue to profit from it. Rupert Hartmoor pretended to be helping Uncle, when really he was stealing important files to sabotage the work!'

'And meanwhile,' added Lizzie, 'they arranged for Meecham to be promoted and called in favours from him. In his position with the Bow Street Runners, Meecham had access to the addresses of those who had taken so many young people after our last case. That was how they always knew the Sons and Daughters were coming. Isn't that so, Meg?'

Meg nodded, arms folded. 'Of course we didn't have a breach of security in our own ranks,' she said, looking up to the gallery of her comrades. 'I should have known. A man in a position of trust, a constable of the law, who should have been protecting the public from crime –'

'Or helping to rescue our young men and women!' rejoined Mrs Sancho.

'– instead was ensuring that his officers were deployed to country houses, ready to arrest Sons and Daughters of Africa when they arrived on rescue missions!' Meg shook her head in disgust.

I stepped in. 'We were surprised that a man who had failed to make any progress with the cases we had brought to him should be promoted. And then I remembered the words we had heard Hartmoor say to Gainsborough that night: "Think of it as a form of promotion. A handshake, a favour, an agreement between gentlemen".'

Whispers of condemnation passed around the room.

'And Lord Mansfield's poisoning?' asked Mr Sancho, moving to seat himself beside Uncle on the chaise longue. 'The Bow Street Runners incriminated my family!'

It was no surprise that Mr Sancho should feel so aggrieved. 'I knew from the beginning that the Sanchos would never have tried to poison Uncle,' I replied. I bit my lip, remembering my doubts about the Sons and Daughters of Africa. 'But Rupert Hartmoor tried to sow suspicion in my mind by suggesting that other members of the Sons and Daughters might resent him.' I looked to Lizzie, who was facing me from the other end of the balcony. 'The Hartmoors have consistently tried to break us apart.'

I took a breath to steady myself. 'Rupert Hartmoor poisoned Uncle's tea by mixing it with extract of foxglove leaves. Uncle felt the impact of the tea on his heart – he suffered palpitations and had to take to his bed. Poisoning designed to look like a natural illness caused by the stress of Uncle's work.'

I blinked back tears, remembering how close Uncle had come to death. 'Hartmoor continued to administer poison to Uncle. And when Uncle fell really ill, in his guise as our friend, Hartmoor boldly offered to call Dr Simpson, not imagining for a minute that Dr Simpson would suspect poisoning. But Dr Simpson had seen digitalis poisoning before. He identified that poisoning had taken place.'

Lizzie moved along the balcony towards me. Heartened, I summoned all the strength I needed to condemn the true criminals. 'Rupert Hartmoor panicked and called in Meecham to implicate the Sanchos. He persuaded Meecham to announce that the peppermint tea was responsible for the poisoning. But the poison caused Uncle to fall ill the morning after the portrait was stolen. Which was *before* the peppermint tea came into the house! Suddenly there was chaos. SDOA members were being arrested left, right and centre, and all bonds of trust between us were seemingly broken.'

I grasped Lizzie's hand tightly. 'Seemingly, but not truly.'

Lizzie took hold of my other hand and we faced each other squarely.

I held her eyes with mine. 'They have done everything they could to come between us and our families, between us and our freedom,' I said. Then I turned to the room, to the Daughters of Africa lined up on the balcony, to Kofi, Aja and Meg, Brother Cugoano, Joshua and Frances in the room below. 'They have stolen from us, intimidated us, deceived us, poisoned us, incarcerated us.'

'Look at Hartmoor!' Lizzie cried, pointing to the man who glowered silently, Sister Clara's hand clamped firmly on his arm. 'Look at his son. At Meecham! Look at what they have become, at what their greed, their cruelty has driven them to. Power is the deadliest poison of all!'

She turned back to me, her voice low and steady now. 'But those of us who are standing are standing because they have underestimated us. They have underestimated the strength of our community, the bonds between us, and our capacity to make our own freedom. But most of all, they have underestimated the power of our friendship.'

Corruption is a strange thing.

When the magistrates arrived in a Bow Street coach for Hugh and Rupert Hartmoor and Meecham, not one of them resisted arrest. Maybe all three believed that they would not spend long in prison. That the system they had all manipulated to their own ends would work in their favour once more and they would soon walk free. Or maybe each man was tired of living life with a bitter taste in their mouth and a stone lodged in their heart.

When it was his turn to be bundled into the Bow Street coach, Meecham refused to look the arresting officer in the eye. I could not help but wonder: how many officers would have chosen Meecham's path if it had been offered to them?

Chapter Forty-Three

You are cordially invited to the Grand Exhibition
at the Royal Academy for a private view of the
work of Miss Jane Harry,
winner of this year's Portrait Prize.

Works on display include the renowned
Sancho–Mansfield Portrait

Lizzie and I stepped together into the Exhibition Hall, already thronging with Miss Harry's guests, gowned and suited, abuzz with conversation. The sinking sun sent dusk's rays through the high-vaulted room, painting the scene in a soft pink light.

At the far end of the hall, the Sancho-Mansfield Portrait had already drawn a circle of intrigued onlookers. I heaved a sigh of relief. The celebration of unity between our families, Jane Harry's view of a harmonious future, was finally getting the audience it deserved. It was flanked by another painting, curtained, to be revealed later on in the proceedings.

Our families had arrived ahead of us. Aja and Mrs Sancho, each dressed in a rich shade of dark crimson, were deep in animated chatter, while Aunt Betty and Uncle William stood, arm in arm, heads bent together, watching the hall fill with guests. Thanks to one of Aja's tinctures, Uncle William had been growing stronger by the day and this was his first major outing in weeks. Mr Sancho, splendid in matching crimson coat and breeches, was laughing with Gainsborough and Dupont, an arm around each of their shoulders.

'This is more like it!' whispered Lizzie, turning in a circle to take in the array of portraits on the walls.

Miss Harry had created a gallery of portraits of the Sons and Daughters of Africa. The framed paintings covered the walls from floor to ceiling, each of their Black subjects holding court from the centre of the canvas. There was Brother Cugoano, bedecked in an orange coat with silver buttons, a book open on his lap, a quill pen in his hand. There was Sister Clara, gowned in royal blue, one hand on her hip, wearing a proud smile.

There was Joshua, resplendent in his silver coat, seated on a dapple grey stallion. On a partner panel, Lizzie's sister Frances in a white gown with lavender stripes, arms filled with books, eyeing the viewer with a piercing gaze.

And there was Meg. Captain Meg. Buttoned up in a black military jacket, shoulders set, arms folded across her chest, head held high, ebony eyes gleaming.

Everywhere you looked, brothers and sisters shone centre stage, dressed in dazzling colours, posing proud.

'There's Kofi!' said Lizzie, nodding to where Kofi stood contemplating a painting.

He greeted each of us with a swift tight hug. We turned then, all three, to the picture on the wall. A family portrait: Kofi and his mother. Aja was seated on a chair, Kofi standing behind her, his hand on her shoulder. Both were clothed in white robes, edged with geometrical patterns in magenta, emerald, gold and black. On her lap, Aja held another painting: a head and shoulders portrait of man, the smile on his lips somehow familiar.

'Kofi! Your father?' Lizzie said, turning to him.

Kofi nodded, his eyes luminous. 'His name was Ade.'

Even when our loved ones are gone from us, we can keep them close in some way. If we are lucky, we might have a painting, a letter, something tangible to remember them by. Or we might simply have our own memories to cherish.

My memories of my own mother and father were cloudy: mere impressions. But they were all I had. Perhaps, I mused, if I were to write them down, they would take on new substance, new life.

Mrs Sancho had once told me that in order to move forward, you had to look back first and face your past.

Only then could you really step into your future.

Sankofa, she called it.

From the front of the room, the sound of a fork tapping on glass. The speeches were about to begin.

'What will you do now?' I asked Kofi as we made our way to the front of the room.

He threw me a shy smile. 'Mama and I have started making herbal remedies together,' he replied, with a hint of pride. 'Mrs Sancho has agreed to stock them in the shop until we can open our own apothecary's!'

What did my own future hold, I wondered.

'Thank you all so much for coming!' said Miss Harry, beckoning us all closer. She was dressed in a tightly fitted gold silk gown, with white lace edging, her magnificent cloud of golden hair brushed out around her face, her green eyes glowing with pleasure. 'I never dreamed I'd be standing here one day, presenting my own exhibition!' she said breathlessly, hands clasped in front of her chest.

'Hear, hear!' cried Mrs Sancho, to whoops and whistles of encouragement.

'But these women and these men,' Miss Harry continued, extending her hand towards the crowd, 'those you see here in the hall around you, and pictured on the walls, are the real stars of the show. To them we owe our freedom and our future!'

A round of applause went up around the room.

'I'm delighted to finally be able to present the Sancho-Mansfield Portrait, which has been . . . in "hiding" for some time! And in addition,' she said, turning to Lizzie and me, 'I am thrilled to unveil a work in honour of my new friends.'

Jane Harry pulled on the cord to reveal a double portrait of myself and Lizzie, standing back to back, our heads turned to eye the viewer directly. Lizzie held a magnifying glass to her face: I clasped a set of notes to my chest. Underneath, our agency motto was engraved:

Lizzie AND **Belle**

Agents of History, Partners in Mystery,
Sisters in solving crime

Lizzie gasped softly beside me. There we were, caught in the act of 'detection'! Just as we saw ourselves, exactly as we wished to be seen.

'Ladies and gentlemen!' cried Miss Harry. 'Please join me in toasting – Lizzie and Belle!'

The guests raised their glasses. 'Lizzie and Belle!'

'Ready?' Lizzie whispered.

I took hold of her hand. 'With you? Always!'

We stepped up on to the stage together as the crowd applauded. I looked out at our friends, our families, our brothers and sisters in arms, with gratitude.

There had been times on this journey when I had doubted whether we would succeed, or even survive. Whether we would ever be able to overcome the forces that threatened us from the shadows: the invisible powers of the Brotherhood of Masters.

Lizzie had taught me the meaning of true courage. She had shown me what it meant to never give up on a loved one, no matter how difficult the circumstances.

And I knew now that neither Lizzie nor I would have been able to pull any of this off alone. It was our partnership that was crucial. Our ability to work together, our trust in each other, our willingness to lift each other up when we fell.

Miss Harry nodded to the musicians seated at the back of the hall. On cue they lifted their instruments and started up a gavotte. With a great rustle of silk, the room swished into two waves like the parting of an ocean. Lizzie and I faced each other then, she on one side, I on the other.

One side of the room bowed. The other returned the gesture with a deep curtsey. Then we all moved together as one: stately, serene, bound together by the beat of the music.

Aunt Betty and Uncle William, stepping with care,

guiding each other back and forth with a tenderness developed over decades.

Mr and Mrs Sancho, their expressions grave, danced with the deliberate, precise wisdom of elders.

Frances and Joshua moved in a looser mood, swinging towards and away from each other, turning their heads slowly to hold each other's gaze as they twisted and dipped in time with the tune.

And Lizzie and myself. Friends bound closer together now by the very challenges that had threatened to drive us apart. Bound, not by chains, not by fear, nor even by duty, but by love.

What is the meaning of family after all? The people with whom we share blood? Or those with whom we spend our days, regardless of our lineage by birth? Those with whom we choose to be, to whom we return again and again, no matter what life throws our way?

I told you at the beginning of this story that what had transformed me was friendship.

I trust you will agree that our story reveals this to be true.

But as Lizzie and I stepped and spun slowly around each other now, mutually enchanted by the magic of the music, joined in joy by the meeting of palms in the space between us, I knew with absolute certainty that what we now shared was something unmistakably, undeniably deeper than any ordinary friendship.

What we shared, was sisterhood.

Acknowledgements

The Lizzie and Belle Mysteries: Portraits and Poison is about the ways in which friends can become family.

First of all my thanks to my gorgeous family for their unending love, encouragement and support, and for the joyful journey of our family life! Richard, Felix, Frankie: you are my world.

My humble thanks to our extended family and our family of friends who have followed me faithfully on the Lizzie and Belle journey!

Thank you to my fellow writers and educators for supporting a 'newbie' writer on the block with shoutouts and shared discussions. Stronger together.

Thank you to my dear friend Nicole-Rachelle Moore at the British Library and Nadia Joseph at New Beacon Books for championing The Lizzie and Belle Mysteries with love and affection.

At Farshore, thanks to Pippa Poole and her team for shining a light on Lizzie and Belle and introducing them to many readers!

Thank you to amazing illustrator Simone Douglas and designer Olivia Adams for bringing Lizzie and Belle and their world to life in glorious detail! Simone, your beautiful work is an inspiration to me as a writer and to our readers.

Sincere and heartfelt thanks to my outstanding editorial team: Sarah Levison, Aleena Hasan and Lucy Courtenay for their energy and their enthusiasm, their passion and their patience, and their belief in the book and in me. What a journey!

Thank you Jasmine Richards at Storymix for always being there to listen, to advise, to champion the work. I am truly grateful for your wise soul, your youthful spirit, your warm heart. This partnership lives on. . .

And finally, I give thanks to my mother, for her loving, laughing, fighting spirit, and to my father, a gentle soul with outstanding artistic talent. The work is always for you two.

A Note on
Portraits and Poison

I love visiting art galleries. Many of them are free to enter and they are brilliant places for research for writing! We can learn so much about our history by looking at paintings from the past. Have you noticed how portraits are often carefully constructed? Clothing, body language, facial expressions, gestures and objects in a painting can all tell a story about the sitter, the artist and the society within which the painting was created.

When I see images of Black people in paintings from the past, I find myself drawn towards them as though by an invisible, mysterious force. I want to know who those people were, what their lives might have been like, why they have been depicted in a particular way, and how they felt whilst they 'sat' for the painting.

When readers ask me about my inspirations for writing, one firmly imprinted in my memory is my first sighting of Dido Belle's portrait at Kenwood House. Dido Belle – like Ignatius Sancho – had her portrait painted at a time when British artists rarely depicted Black people as dignified subjects in their own right.

In the portrait, Dido's eyes are on a level with her cousin Elizabeth's. Though she is dressed in a stereotypical 'exotic' costume often given to Black people to wear for Georgian paintings, Dido eyes the viewer directly, wearing an intriguing smile and pointing to her cheek.

Is she inviting us to consider the colour of her skin?

Is she rushing out of the painting?

What does this painting tell us about this young woman? And whose 'version' of her does it represent?

But Dido's portrait is more an exception than a rule. British art from the 17th and 18th centuries reveals a troubling pattern in the ways in which Black people were represented by white artists. And, more often than not, those Black sitters are not named in the paintings in which they appeared: as though their lives did not matter.

Now more work is being done to discover more about the lives of the Black people who appear in these paintings, to recover the details of their lives alongside those of their white counterparts. Each of us can play our part by being curious and by carrying out our own research. And, crucially, there are a number of African heritage artists creating new work that speaks back to eighteenth century art, centring Black people and restoring their power in portraiture.

Like *Drama and Danger* before it, *Portraits and Poison* is a work of fiction: some of the characters are based on real historical figures, but all of the characters as depicted here are works of my own imagination.

But embedded within this work of fiction are truths about the British past that are not often discussed openly: the holding of people as enslaved servants on British soil; the ways in which people sought their freedom by running away – well-documented in 17th and 18th century newspapers; and of course the placing of young Black boys and girls, women and men, in the corners of portraits of their well-to-do and wealthy white counterparts.

It is important that we acknowledge these troubling stories in order to better understand our history. Amongst them we also find inspiring examples of Black resistance in those who rose up and revolted, those who ran away, and those who wrote their life stories.

Nowadays you don't have to be a wealthy landowner to have your portrait out there for people to see. In a digital age when we are producing more images, photographs, portraits and self-portraits than ever before, how do we take care of the ways in which we are represented out in the world?

How do we see ourselves?

How do we wish to be seen?

And what role do portraits have now in the shaping of identity?

Join **Lizzie and Belle** in
their first thrilling adventure!

Read on for a sneak peek . . .

To begin with, there was nothing out of the ordinary about the night of Friday 11th April 1777. It was just like any other Friday night in Covent Garden. Or so it seemed. The market square swirled with street traders selling flowers and fruit in all colours of the rainbow. Coaches and carriages passed back and forth, stopping every now and then to let the horses drop their manure. Shoppers hurried along the cobblestones, pulling their coats tighter about them as the sun sank slowly behind the skyline of colonnades and spires that graced the Thames.

If someone had been looking very carefully, however, they might have noticed a tall, cloaked figure, skulking in a shadowed doorway as the crowds passed by. If they had continued to pay close attention, they might have seen the figure disappear into the back door of the Theatre Royal at Drury Lane.

Someone extremely perceptive would have also observed a smaller figure – a girl – leaving Madame Hassan's Haberdashery on Maiden Lane, clutching a package and scurrying through Covent Garden Market as though her life depended on it. And if they had followed that girl, they would have seen her tearing down the Strand, along Whitehall and into Charles Street, making a beeline for Ignatius Sancho's Tea Shop.

Right. So, I should let you know that that girl is me. Lizzie Sancho, twelve years old, Londoner. I am definitely not your typical eighteenth-century girl. *Who is?* I hear you ask. But what I mean is, I'm not interested in attending society balls or wearing the latest fashions or reading the gossip columns in the newspapers. And personally, I don't know many girls that are interested in those things. But then, maybe I don't move in the right circles.

I spend most of my time helping out with the family business. We own a grocery store in the heart of Westminster that doubles as a tea shop and what my father likes to call a 'literary salon'.

And here he is! May I present Ignatius Sancho? Gentleman. Grocer. Writer. Composer. Abolitionist.

He used to work as a butler for an aristocratic family and he knows a lot of people. I mean, a *lot*. Actors, artists, writers, musicians: you name it! The shop is always crammed with people huddled in corners, swapping stories, planning protests, hatching plots, reciting poetry, sharing secrets. A proper hotbed of news and information.

Helping out in the shop is how I have developed my extraordinary powers of observation. You see, I have a trick – a gift, Mama calls it – of noticing things that other people don't. I can tell all sorts of things about someone just by the way they enter a room, or eat an apple, or ask me for directions in the street. You'd be amazed at what you can learn about life just by observing people closely. And eavesdropping, of course.

But I digress. Back to Papa.

So, his latest obsession is acting. He quotes Shakespeare at me and our family on a daily basis – sometimes hourly, no joke.

'Everything one could wish to learn about human behaviour,' he announces, 'we could learn from William Shakespeare!'

Tonight he will take to the stage to play Othello at the Theatre Royal, Drury Lane. Othello is one of Shakespeare's very few Black characters. A military general, respected by his colleagues and those he commands, and married to Desdemona, a young white woman. The play is almost one hundred and eighty years old, and has been performed many times, but the character of Othello has yet to be played by a Black man on the British stage. Can you believe it?

When Papa first told me that, some months back, I actually thought I'd misheard him. In fact, I accidentally spat out my tea.

'What?' I spluttered, spraying tiny drops of hot water in a shower of surprise.

'Never once yet, dear Lizzie,' Papa replied, in his rolling baritone. 'Until now.'

I mopped the table surreptitiously with my sleeve. 'But that's ridiculous, Papa! Why not?'

'That, dear heart, is a very good question,' he replied, refilling my cup with Orange Pekoe tea. 'A very good question indeed.'